Praise for Colin Dexter
and his Inspector Morse series

"[Morse is] the most prickly, conceited, and genuinely brilliant detective since Hercule Poirot."
—*The New York Times Book Review*

"Dexter excels in constructing clever plots full of erudite clues and droll characterizations."
—*San Francisco Chronicle*

"You don't really know Morse until you've read him. . . . Viewers who have enjoyed British actor John Thaw as Morse in the PBS *Mystery!* anthology series should welcome the deeper character development in Dexter's novels."
—*Chicago Sun-Times*

"It is a delight to watch this brilliant, quirky man deduce."
—*Minneapolis Star &Tribune*

"A masterful crime writer whom few others match."
—*Publishers Weekly*

By Colin Dexter:

LAST BUS TO WOODSTOCK*
LAST SEEN WEARING*
THE SILENT WORLD OF NICHOLAS QUINN*
SERVICE OF ALL THE DEAD*
THE DEAD OF JERICHO*
THE RIDDLE OF THE THIRD MILE*
THE SECRET OF ANNEXE 3*
THE WENCH IS DEAD*
THE JEWEL THAT WAS OURS*
THE WAY THROUGH THE WOODS*
THE DAUGHTERS OF CAIN*
MORSE'S GREATEST MYSTERY and Other
   Stories*
DEATH IS NOW MY NEIGHBOR*
THE WENCH IS DEAD*

*Published by Ivy Books

> Thou hast committed—
> Fornication; but that was in another country,
> And besides, the wench is dead.
> (CHRISTOPHER MARLOWE, *The Jew of Malta*)

THE WENCH
IS DEAD

Colin Dexter

IVY BOOKS • NEW YORK

Ivy Books
Published by The Ballantine Publishing Group
Copyright © 1989 by Colin Dexter

www.randomhouse.com/BB/

Library of Congress Catalog Card Number: 98-94258

ISBN 0-8041-1889-2

This edition published by arrangement with St. Martin's Press.

Manufactured in the United States of America

First Ivy Books Edition: June 1999

10 9 8 7 6 5 4 3 2 1

For Harry Judge, lover of canals, who introduced me to *The Murder of Christine Collins*, a fascinating account of an early Victorian murder, by John Godwin. To both I am deeply indebted. (Copies of John Godwin's publication are obtainable through the Divisional Librarian, Stafford Borough Library.)

Acknowledgements

The author and publishers wish to thank the following who have kindly given permission for use of copyright materials:

Map of the Oxford Canal reproduced by permission of Oxfordshire Museum Services;

Century Hutchinson Limited for extracts from *Adventures in Wonderland* by David Grayson;

Faber and Faber Ltd. for extracts from "Little Gidding" from *Four Quartets* by T.S. Eliot;

David Higham Associates Limited on behalf of Dorothy L. Sayers for extracts from *The Murder of Julia Wallace*, published by Gollancz;

Methuen London Limited for extracts from *A Man's a Man* by Bertolt Brecht;

Oxfordshire Health Authority for extracts from *Handbook for Patients and Visitors*;

Oxford Illustrated Press for extracts from *The Erosion of Oxford* by James Stevens Curl;

E. O. Parrott for extracts;

THE OXFORD CANAL

Legend:
- Oxford Canal main line
- Oxford Canal old line
- Other navigable waterways
- Oxford Canal old line
- Locks

Coventry Canal
HAWKESBURY JUNCTION
Longford Old Junction
Hawkesbury Stop Lock
WYKEN COLLIERY BRANCHES
CHOPSFORD VALLEY AQUEDUCT
STRETTON WHARF
BRINKLOW ARM
BRINKLOW AQUEDUCT
COVENTRY
BROWNSOVER FEEDER ARM
NEWBOLD TUNNELS
RUGBY WHARF
CLIFTON WHARF
Hillmorton Locks
RUGBY
Grand Junction (now Grand Union) Canal
BRAUNSTON JUNCTION
Warwick & Napton (now Grand Union) Canal
WOLFHAMPCOTE LOOP & OLD TUNNEL
NAPTON JUNCTION
Napton Locks
Green's Lock — Arm to old Engine House
Napton Top Lock — Marston Doles Lock
WORMLEIGHTON LOOP
SUMMIT LEVEL
WORMLEIGHTON RES.
BODDINGTON RESERVOIR
PENNY COMPTON CUTTING
Claydon Locks
CLATTERCOTE RESERVOIR
Elkington's Lock
Varney's Lock
Broadmoor Lock
Cropredy Lock
Slat Mill Lock
Little Bourton or Jobson's Lock
Hardwick or Solman's Lock
Banbury Lock
BANBURY
Grant's Lock
Tarver's or King's Sutton Lock
Nell Bridge Lock
Aynho Weir Lock
N
Somerton Deep Lock
0   Miles   5
0   Km   10
Heyford Common Lock
Allen's or Heyford Mill Lock
Dashwood's Lock
Northbrook Lock
Pigeon or Enson's Mill Lock
Baker's or Gibraltar Lock
Shipton Weir Lock
THRUPP WIDE
Roundham Lock
Kidlington Green Lock
DUKE'S CUT & LOCK
Duke's or Shuttleworth's Lock
Wolvercote Lock
HAYFIELD WHARF
River Thames
HYTHE BRIDGE
NEW ROAD &
Isis or Louse Lock
WORCESTER ST. BASINS
OXFORD

Chapter One

Thought depends absolutely on the stomach; but, in spite of that, those who have the best stomachs are not the best thinkers.

(*Voltaire, in a letter to d'Alembert*)

Intermittently, on the Tuesday, he felt sick. Frequently, on the Wednesday, he *was* sick. On the Thursday, he felt sick frequently, but was actually sick only intermittently. With difficulty, early on the Friday morning—drained, listless, and infinitely weary—he found the energy to drag himself from his bed to the telephone, and seek to apologise to his superiors at Kidlington Police HQ for what was going to be an odds-on non-appearance at the office that late November day.

When he awoke on the Saturday morning, he was happily aware that he was feeling considerably better; and, indeed, as he sat in the kitchen of his

1

bachelor flat in North Oxford, dressed in pyjamas as gaudily striped as a Lido deckchair, he was debating whether his stomach could cope with a wafer of Weetabix—when the phone rang.

"Morse here," he said.

"Good morning, sir." (A pleasing voice!) "If you can hold the line a minute, the Superintendent would like a word with you."

Morse held the line. Little option, was there? No option, really; and he scanned the headlines of *The Times* which had just been pushed through the letter-box in the small entrance hall—late, as usual on Saturdays.

"I'm putting you through to the Superintendent," said the same pleasing voice—"just a moment, please!"

Morse said nothing; but he almost prayed (quite something for a low-church atheist) that Strange would get a move on and come to the phone and say whatever it was he'd got to say . . . The prickles of sweat were forming on his forehead, and his left hand plucked at his pyjama-top pocket for his handkerchief.

"Ah! Morse? Yes? Ah! Sorry to hear you're a bit off-colour, old boy. Lots of it about, you know. The wife's brother had it—when was it now?—fortnight or so back? No! I tell a lie—must have been three weeks, at least. Still, that's neither here nor there, is it?"

In enlarged globules, the prickles of sweat had reformed on Morse's forehead, and he wiped his brow once more as he mumbled a few dutifully appreciative noises into the telephone.

"Didn't get you out of bed, I hope?"

"No—no, sir."

"Good. Good! Thought I'd just have a quick word, that's all. Er . . . Look here, Morse!" (Clearly Strange's thoughts had moved to a conclusion.) "No need for you to come in today—no need at all! Unless you feel suddenly very much better, that is. We can just about cope here, I should think. The cemeteries are full of indispensable men—eh? Huh!"

"Thank you, sir. Very kind of you to ring—I much appreciate it—but I am officially off duty this weekend in any case—"

"Really? Ah! That's good! That's er . . . *very* good, isn't it? Give you a chance to stay in bed."

"Perhaps so, sir," said Morse wearily.

"You say you're *up*, though?"

"Yes, sir!"

"Well you go back to bed, Morse! This'll give you a chance for a jolly good rest—this weekend, I mean—won't it? Just the thing—bit o' rest—when you're feeling a bit off-colour—eh? It's exactly what the quack told the wife's brother—when was it now . . . ?"

Afterwards, Morse thought he remembered concluding this telephone conversation in a seemly manner—with appropriate concern expressed for Strange's convalescent brother-in-law; thought he remembered passing a hand once more over a forehead that now felt very wet and very, very cold—and then taking two or three hugely deep breaths—and then starting to rush for the bathroom . . .

It was Mrs. Green, the charlady who came in on Tuesday and Saturday mornings, who rang treble-nine immediately and demanded an ambulance. She had found her employer sitting with his back to the wall in the entrance-hall: conscious, seemingly sober, and passably presentable, except for the deep-maroon stains down the front of his deckchair pyjamas—stains that in both colour and texture served vividly to remind her of the dregs in the bottom of a coffee percolator. And she knew exactly what *they* meant, because that thoughtlessly cruel doctor had made it quite plain—five years ago now, it had been—that if only she'd called him immediately, Mr. Green might still . . .

"Yes, that's right," she heard herself say—surprisingly, imperiously, in command: "just on the southern side of the Banbury Road roundabout. Yes. I'll be looking out for you."

At 10:15 A.M. that same morning, an only semi-reluctant Morse condescended to be helped into the back of the ambulance, where, bedroom-slippered and with an itchy, grey blanket draped around a clean pair of pyjamas, he sat defensively opposite a middle-aged, uniformed woman who appeared to have taken his refusal to lie down on the stretcher-bed as a personal affront, and who now sullenly and silently pushed a white enamel kidney-bowl into his lap as he vomited copiously and noisily once more, while the ambulance climbed Headly Way, turned left into the grounds of the John Radcliffe Hospital complex, and finally stopped outside the Accident, Casualty, and Emergency Department.

As he lay supine (on a hospital trolley now) it occurred to Morse that he might already have died some half-a-dozen times without anyone recording his departure. But he was always an impatient soul (most particularly in hotels, when awaiting his breakfast); and it might not have been quite as long as he imagined before a white-coated ancillary worker led him in leisurely fashion through a questionnaire that ranged from the names of his next of kin (in Morse's case, now non-existent) to his denominational preferences (equally, alas, now non-existent). Yet once through these initiation rites—once (as it were) he had joined the club and signed the entry forms—Morse found himself the object of considerably increased attention. Dutifully, from somewhere, a young nurse appeared, flipped a watch from her stiffly laundered lapel with her left hand and took his pulse with her right; proceeded to take his blood-pressure, after tightening the black swaddling-bands around his upper-arm with (for Morse) quite needless ferocity; and then committing her findings to a chart (headed MORSE, E.) with such nonchalance as to suggest that only the most dramatic of irregularities could ever give occasion for anxiety. The same nurse finally turned her attention to matters of temperature; and Morse found himself feeling somewhat idiotic as he lay with a thermometer sticking up from his mouth, before its being extracted, its calibrations consulted, its readings apparently unsatisfactory, it being forcefully shaken thrice, as though for a few backhand flicks in a Ping-Pong match, and then being replaced, with all its earlier awkwardness, just underneath his tongue.

"I'm going to survive?" ventured Morse, as the nurse added her further findings to the data on his chart.

"You've got a temperature," replied the uncommunicative teenager.

"I thought *everybody* had got a temperature," muttered Morse.

For the moment, however, the nurse had turned her back on him to consider the latest casualty.

A youth, his legs caked with mud, and most of the rest of him encased in a red-and-black-striped

Rugby jersey, had just been wheeled in—a ghastly looking Cyclopean slit across his forehead. Yet, to Morse, he appeared wholly at his ease as the (same) ancillary worker quizzed him comprehensively about his life-history, his religion, his relatives. And when, equally at his ease, the (same) nurse put him through his paces with stethoscope, watch, and thermometer, Morse could do little but envy the familiarity that was affected forthwith between the young lad and the equally young lass. Suddenly—and almost cruelly—Morse realised that she, that same young lass, had seen him— Morse!—exactly for what he was: a man who'd struggled through life to his early fifties, and who was about to face the slightly *infra-dignitatem* embarrassments of hernias and haemorrhoids, of urinary infections and—yes!—of duodenal ulcers.

The kidney-bowl had been left within easy reach, and Morse was retching violently, if unproductively, when a young houseman (of Morse's age, no more than half) came to stand beside him and to scan the reports of ambulance, administrative staff, and medical personnel.

"You've got a bit of nasty tummy trouble—you realise that?"

Morse shrugged vaguely: "Nobody's really told me anything yet."

"But you wouldn't have to be Sherlock Holmes

to suspect you've got something pretty radically wrong with your innards, would you?"

Morse was about to reply when the houseman continued. "And you've only just come in, I think? If you could give us—Mr., er, *Morse,* is it?—if you give us a chance, we'll try to tell you more about things as soon as we can, OK?"

"I'm all right, really," said the duly chastened Chief Inspector of Police, as he lay back and tried to unloose the knot that had tied itself tight inside his shoulder muscles.

"You're *not* all right, I'm afraid! At best you've got a stomach ulcer that's suddenly decided to burst out bleeding"—Morse experienced a sharp little jerk of alarm somewhere in his diaphragm— "and at worst you've got what we call a 'perforated ulcer'; and if that is the case . . ."

"If that *is* the case . . . ?" repeated Morse weakly. But the young doctor made no immediate answer, and for the next few minutes prodded, squeezed, and kneaded the paunchy flesh around Morse's abdomen.

"Found anything?" queried Morse, with a thin and forced apology for a grin.

"You could well lose a couple of stone. Your liver's enlarged."

"But I thought you just said it was the stomach!"

"Oh yes, it is! You've had a stomach haemorrhage."

"What's—what's that got to do with my liver?"

"Do you drink a lot, Mr. Morse?"

"Well, most people have a drink or two most days, don't they?"

"Do you drink a *lot*?" (The same words—a semi-tone of exasperation lower.)

As non-commitally as his incipient panic would permit, Morse shrugged his shoulders once more: "I like a glass of beer, yes."

"How many pints do you drink a week?"

"A week?" squeaked Morse, his face clouding over like that of a child who has just been given a complex problem in mental multiplication.

"A day, then?" suggested the houseman helpfully.

Morse divided by three: "Two or three, I suppose."

"Do you drink spirits?"

"Occasionally."

"What spirits do you drink?"

Morse shrugged his tautened shoulders once again: "Scotch—sometimes I treat myself to a drop of Scotch."

"How long would a bottle of Scotch last you?"

"Depends how big it was."

But Morse immediately saw that his attempt at

humour was ill appreciated; and he swiftly multi-
plied by three: "Week—ten days—about that."

"How many cigarettes do you smoke a day?"

"Eight . . . ten?" replied Morse, getting the hang
of things now and smoothly dividing by three.

"Do you ever take any exercise—walking, jog-
ging, cycling, squash . . . ?"

But before Morse could switch back to his tables,
he reached for the kidney-bowl that had been left
within reach. And as he vomited, this time produc-
tively, the houseman observed with some alarm the
coffee-grounds admixed with the tell-tale brightly
crimsoned specks of blood—blood that was de-
oxygenated daily with plentiful nicotine and liber-
ally lubricated with alcohol.

For some while after these events, Morse's mind
was somewhat hazy. Later, however, he could recall
a nurse bending over him—the same young nurse as
earlier; and he could remember the beautifully
manicured fingers on her left hand as she flipped
the watch out again into her palm; could almost follow her thoughts as with contracted brow she
squinted at the disturbing equation between his
half-minute pulse-rate and the thirty-second span
upon her watch . . .

At this point Morse knew that the Angel of
Death had fluttered its wings above his head; and he
felt a sudden frisson of fear, as for the first time in
his life he began to think of dying. For in his mind's

eye, though just for a second or two, he thought he almost caught sight of the laudatory obituary, the creditable paragraph.

Chapter Two

Do you know why we are more fair and just towards the dead? We are not obliged to them, we can take our time, we can fit in the paying of respects between a cocktail party and an affectionate mistress—in our spare time.

(*Albert Camus,* The Fall)

When Morse awoke the following morning, he was aware of a grey dawn through the window of the small ward, to his left; and of a clock showing 4:50 A.M. on the wall above the archway to his right, through which he could see a slimly attractive nurse, sitting in a pool of light behind a desk, and writing in a large book. Was she writing, Morse wondered, about *him*? If so, there would be remarkably little to say; for apart from one very brief bout of vomiting in the small hours, he had felt, quite genuinely, so very much better; and had required no further attention. The tubing strapped to

13

his right wrist, and stretching up to the saline-drip bottle hooked above his bed, was still dragging uncomfortably against his skin most of the time, as if the needle had been stuck in slightly off-centre; but he'd determined to make no mention of such a minor irritant. The awkward apparatus rendered him immobile, of course—at least until he had mastered the skills of the young man from the adjacent bed who had spent most of the previous evening wandering freely (as it seemed) all over the hospital, holding his own drip high above his head like some Ethiopian athlete brandishing the Olympic torch. Morse had felt most self-conscious when circumstances utterly beyond his control had finally induced him to beg for a "bottle." Yet—thus far—he had been spared the undignified palaver of the dreaded "pan"; and he trusted that his lack of solid nutriment during the preceding days would be duly acknowledged with some reciprocal inactivity by his bowels. And so far so good!

The nurse was talking earnestly to a slightly built, fresh-faced young houseman, his white coat reaching almost to his ankles, a stethoscope hooked into his right-hand pocket. And soon the two of them were walking, quietly, unfussily, into the ward where Morse lay; then disappearing behind the curtains (drawn across the previous evening) of the bed diagonally opposite.

When he'd first been wheeled into the ward,

Morse had noticed the man who occupied that
bed—a proud-looking man, in his late seventies,
perhaps, with an Indian Army moustache, and a
thin thatch of pure-white hair. At that moment of
entry, for a second or two, the old warrior's watery-
pale eyes had settled on Morse's face, seeming almost to convey some faint message of hope and
comradeship. And indeed the dying old man would
certainly have wished the new patient well, had he
been able to articulate his intent; but the rampag-
ing septicaemia which had sent a bright-pink suffusion to his waxen cheeks had taken from him all the
power of speech.

It was 5:20 A.M. when the houseman emerged
from behind the curtains; 5:30 A.M. when the swiftly
summoned porters had wheeled the dead man
away. And when, exactly half an hour later, the full
lights flickered on in the ward, the curtains round
the bed of the late Colonel Wilfrid Deniston, OBE,
MC, were standing open, in their normal way, to reveal the newly laundered sheets, with the changed
blankets professionally mitred at the foot. Had
Morse known how the late Colonel could not abide
a chord of Wagner he would have been somewhat
aggrieved; yet had he known how the Colonel had
committed to memory virtually the whole poetic
corpus of A. E. Housman, he would have been most
gratified.

At 6:45 A.M. Morse was aware of considerable

activity in the immediate environs of the ward, although initially he could see no physical evidence of it: voices, clinking of crockery, squeaking of ill-oiled wheels—and finally Violet, a happily countenanced and considerably overweight West Indian woman hove into view pushing a tea-trolley. This was the occasion, clearly, for a pre-dawn beverage, and how Morse welcomed it! For the first time in the past few days he was conscious of a positive appetite for food and drink; and already, and with envy, he had surveyed the jugs of water and bottles of squash that stood on the bedside tables of his fellow-patients, though for some reason not on the table of the man immediately opposite, one Walter Greenaway, above whose bed there hung a rectangular plaque bearing the sad little legend NIL BY MOUTH.

"Tea or coffee, Mr. Greenaway?"

"I'll just settle for a large gin-and-tonic, if that's all right by you."

"Ice and lemon?"

"No ice, thank you: it spoils the gin."

Violet moved away massively to the next bed, leaving Mr. Greenaway sans ice, sans everything. Yet the perky sixty-odd-year-old appeared far from mortified by his exclusion from the proceedings, and winked happily across at Morse.

"All right, chief?"

"On the mend," said Morse cautiously.

"Huh! That's exactly what the old Colonel used to say: 'On the mend.' Poor old boy!"

"I see," said Morse, with some unease.

After Greenaway's eyes had unclouded from their appropriate respect for the departed Colonel, Morse continued the dialogue.

"No tea for you, then?"

Greenaway shook his head. "They know best, though, don't they?"

"They do?"

"Wonderful—the doctors here! And the nurses!"

Morse nodded, hoping indeed that it might be so.

"Same trouble as me?" enquired Greenaway confidentially.

"Pardon?"

"Stomach, is it?"

"Ulcer—so they say."

"Mine's perforated!" Greenaway proclaimed this fact with a certain grim pride and satisfaction, as though a combination of the worst of disorders with the best of physicians was a cause for considerable congratulation. "They're operating on me at ten o'clock—that's why I'm not allowed a drink, see?"

"Oh!" For a few seconds Morse found himself almost wishing he could put in some counter-claim for a whole gutful of mighty ulcers that were not only perforated but pierced and punctured into the bargain. A more important matter, however, was now demanding his attention, for Violet had effected a U-turn and was (at last!) beside his bed.

She greeted her new charge with a cheerful grin. "Morning, Mr., er" (consulting the Biro'd letters on the name-tab) "Mr. Morse!"

"Good morning!" replied Morse. "I'll have some coffee, please—two spoonfuls of sugar."

"My, my! *Two—sugars!*" Violet's eyes almost soared out of their whitened sockets towards the ceiling; then she turned to share the private joke with the grinning Greenaway.

"Now, look you here!" (reverting to Morse): "You can't have no coffee nor no tea nor no sugar neither. Oh right?" She wagged a brown forefinger at a point somewhere above the bed; and twisting his neck Morse could see, behind his saline apparatus, a rectangular plaque bearing the sad little legend NIL BY MOUTH.

Chapter Three

> Flowers, writing materials, and books are always wel-
> come gifts for patients; but if you wish to bring food
> or drink, do ask the Sister, and she will tell you what is
> advisable.
>
> (*Oxford Health Authority,* Handbook
> for Patients and Visitors)

Detective Sergeant Lewis came into the ward just
after seven o'clock that Sunday evening, clutching
a Sainsbury carrier-bag with the air of a slightly
guilty man walking through the Customs' shed; and
at the sight of his old partner, Morse felt very glad,
and just a little lachrymose.

"How come you knew I was here?"

"I'm a detective, sir—remember?"

"They phoned you, I suppose."

"The Super. He said you sounded awful poorly
when he rang yesterday morning. So he sent Dixon
round, but you'd just been carried off in the

ambulance. So he rang me and said I might like to see if the NHS is still up to scratch—see if you wanted anything."

"Something like a bottle of Scotch, you mean?"

Lewis ignored the pleasantry: "I'd've come in last night, but they said you weren't to have visitors— only close relatives."

"I'll have you know I'm not quite your 'Orphan Annie,' Lewis. I've got a great-aunt up in Alnwick somewhere."

"Bit of a long way for her to come, sir."

"Especially at ninety-seven . . ."

"Not a bad fellow, Strange, is he?" suggested Lewis, after a slightly awkward little pause.

"Not when you get to know him, I suppose," admitted Morse.

"Would you say *you've* got to know him?"

Morse shook his head.

"Well?" said Lewis briskly. "How *are* things? What do they say's the trouble?"

"Trouble? No trouble! It's just a case of mistaken identity."

Lewis grinned. "Seriously, though?"

"Seriously? Well they've put me on some great big round white pills that cost a couple of quid a time, so the nurses say. Do you realise you can get a very decent little bottle of Claret for that price?"

"What about the food—is that all right?"

"Food? *What* food? Except for the pills they haven't given me a thing."

"No drink, either?"

"Are you trying to set back my medical progress, Lewis?"

"Is that what—what *that* means?" Lewis jerked his eyes upwards to the fateful warning above the bed.

"That's just precautionary," said Morse, with unconvincing nonchalance.

Lewis's eyes jerked, downwards this time, towards the carrier-bag.

"Come on, Lewis! What have you got in there?"

Lewis reached inside the bag and brought out a bottle of lemon-and-barley water, and was most pleasantly surprised to witness the undisguised delight on Morse's face.

"It was just that the missus thought—well, you know, you wouldn't be allowed to drink—to drink anything else much."

"*Very* kind of her! You just tell her that the way things are I'd rather have a bottle of that stuff than a whole crate of whisky."

"You don't mean that, do you, sir?"

"Doesn't stop you telling her, though, does it?"

"And here's a book," added Lewis, withdrawing one further item from the bag—a book entitled *Scales of Injustice: A Comparative Study of Crime*

*and its Punishment as Recorded in the County of
Shropshire, 1842–1852.*

Morse took the thick volume and surveyed its inordinately lengthy title, though without any obvious enthusiasm. "Mm! Looks a fairly interesting work."

"You don't mean that, do you?"

"No," said Morse.

"It's a sort of family heirloom and the missus just thought—"

"You tell that wonderful missus of yours that I'm very pleased with it."

"Perhaps you'll do me a favour and leave it in the hospital library when you come out."

Morse laughed quietly; and Lewis was strangely gratified by his chief's reactions, and smiled to himself.

He was still smiling when an extraordinarily pretty young nurse, with a freckled face and mahogany-highlighted hair, came to Morse's bedside, waved an admonitory finger at him, and showed her white and beautifully regular teeth in a dumbshow of disapproval as she pointed to the lemon-and-barley bottle which Morse had placed on his locker-top. Morse, in turn, nodded his full appreciation of the situation and showed his own reasonably regular, if rather off-white, teeth as he mouthed a silent "OK."

"Who's that?" whispered Lewis, when she had passed upon her way.

"That, Lewis, is the Fair Fiona. Lovely, don't you think? I sometimes wonder how the doctors manage to keep their dirty hands off her."

"Perhaps they don't."

"I thought you'd come in here to cheer me up!"

But for the moment good cheer seemed in short supply. The ward sister (whom Lewis had not noticed as he'd entered—merely walked straight through, like everyone else, as he'd thought) had clearly been keeping her dragon's eye on events in general, and in particular on events around the bed where the dehydrated Chief Inspector lay. To which bed, with purposeful stride, she now took the few steps needed from the vantage point behind the main desk. Her left hand immediately grasped the offending bottle on the locker-top, while her eyes fixed unblinkingly upon the luckless Lewis.

"We have our regulations in this hospital—a copy of them is posted just outside the ward. So I shall be glad if you follow these regulations and report to me or whoever's in charge if you intend to visit again. It's absolutely vital that we follow a routine here—try to understand that! Your friend here is quite poorly, and we're all trying our vairy best to see that he gets well again quickly. Now we canna do that if you are going to bring in anything *you* think might do him good, because you'd bring in all the *wrong* things, OK? I'm sure you appreciate what I'm saying."

She had spoken in a soft Scots accent, this grimly visaged, tight-lipped sister, a silver buckle clasped around her dark-blue uniform; and Lewis, the colour tidally risen under his pale cheeks, looked wretchedly uncomfortable as she turned away—and was gone. Even Morse, for a few moments, appeared strangely cowed and silent.

"Who's that?" asked Lewis (for the second time that evening).

"You have just had an encounter with the embittered soul of our ward sister—devoted to an ideal of humourless efficiency: a sort of Calvinistic Thatcherite."

"And what she says . . . ?"

Morse nodded. "She is, Lewis, in charge; as I think you probably gathered."

"Doesn't have to be so *sharp*, does she?"

"*Forget* it, Lewis! She's probably disappointed in her love-life or something. Not surprising with a face—"

"What's her name?"

"They call her 'Nessie.'"

"Was she born near the Loch?"

"*In* it, Lewis."

The two men laughed just a little; yet the incident had been unpleasant and Lewis in particular found it difficult to put it behind him. For a further five minutes he quizzed Morse quietly about the other patients; and Morse told him of the dawn departure of the ex-Indian-Army man. For still another five minutes, the two men exchanged words about Police HQ at Kidlington; about the Lewis family; about the less-than-sanguine prospects of Oxford United in the current soccer campaign. But nothing could quite efface the fact that "that bloody sister" (as Morse referred to her) had cast a darkling shadow over the evening visit; had certainly cast a shadow over Lewis. And Morse himself was suddenly feeling hot and sweaty, and (yes, if he were honest) just a fraction wearied of the conversation.

"I'd better be off then, sir."

"What else have you got in that bag?"

"Nothing—"

"Lewis! My stomach may be out of order for the minute but there's nothing wrong with my bloody ears!"

Slowly the dark clouds began to lift for Lewis, and when, after prolonged circumspection, he decided that the Customs Officer was momentarily off her guard, he withdrew a small, flattish bottle, wrapped in soft, dark-blue tissue-paper—much the colour of Nessie's uniform.

"But not until it's *official* like!" hissed Lewis, palming the gift surreptitiously into Morse's hand beneath the bedclothes.

"Bells?" asked Morse.

Lewis nodded.

It was a happy moment.

* * *

For the present, however, the attention of all was diverted by another bell that sounded from somewhere, and visitors began to stand and prepare for their departure: a few, perhaps with symptoms of reluctance; but the majority with signs of only partially concealed relief. As Lewis himself rose to take his leave, he dipped his hand once more into the carrier-bag and produced his final offering: a paperback entitled *The Blue Ticket*, with a provocative picture of an economically clad nymphet on the cover.

"I thought—I thought you might enjoy something a little bit lighter, sir. The missus doesn't know—"

"I hope she's never found you reading this sort of rubbish, Lewis!"

"Haven't read it *yet*, sir."

"Well, the, er, title's a bit shorter than the other thing . . ."

Lewis nodded, and the two friends shared a happy grin.

"Time to go, I'm afraid!" The Fair Fiona was smiling down at them, especially (it seemed) smiling down at Lewis, for whom every cloud was suddenly lifted from the weather-chart. As for Morse, he was glad to be alone again; and when the ward finally cleared of its last visitor, the hospital-system

smoothly, inexorably, reorientated itself once more
to the care and treatment of the sick.

It was only after further testings of pulse and
blood-pressure, after the administration of further
medicaments, that Morse had the opportunity (unobserved) of reading the blurb of the second work
of literature (well, literature of a sort) which was
now in his possession:

Diving into the water, young Steve Mingella had
managed to pull the little girl's body on to the
hired yacht and to apply to her his clumsy
version of the kiss-of-life. Miraculously, the six-
year-old had survived, and for a few days Steve
was the toast of the boat clubs along the Florida
Keys. After his return to New York he received a
letter—and inside the letter a ticket—from the
young girl's father, the playboy proprietor of
the city's most exclusive, expensive, and exotic
night-spot, a club specialising in the wildest
sexual fantasies. The book opens as Steve treads
diffidently across the thick carpeted entrance of
that erotic wonderland, and shows to the topless
blonde seated at Reception the ticket he has
received—*a ticket coloured deepest blue* . . .

Chapter Four

> My evening visitors, if they cannot see the clock, should find the time in my face.
>
> (*Emerson*, Journals)

Half an hour after Lewis's departure, Fiona came again to Morse's bedside and asked him to unfasten his pyjama bottoms, to turn over on his left side, and to expose his right buttock. Which orders having been obeyed (as Morse used to say when he studied the Classics), the unsmiling Nessie was summoned to insert a syringe of colourless liquid into his flank. This insertion (he could see nothing over his right shoulder) seemed to Morse to have been effected with less than professional finesse; and he heard himself grunt "Christ!" when the plunger was pressed, his body twitching involuntarily as what felt like a bar of iron was implanted into his backside.

"You'll feel a wee bit sleepy," was the laconic

comment of the Loch Ness Monster; and Fiona was left to pour some disinfectant on to a piece of gauze, which she proceeded to rub vigorously across and around the punctured area.

"She'd have landed a top job in Buchenwald, that woman!" said Morse. But from the uncomprehending look on her face, he suddenly realised that Nazi concentration camps were as far back in the young nurse's past as the relief of Mafeking was in his own; and he felt his age. It was forty-four years now since the end of the Second World War . . . and this young . . . nurse . . . could only be . . . Morse was conscious of feeling very weary, very tired. "What I mean is . . ." (Morse pulled his pyjama bottoms up with some difficulty) ". . . she's so . . . sharp!" Yes, Lewis had used that word.

"Did you realise that was my very first injection? Sorry if it hurt a bit—I'll get better."

"I thought it was . . ."

"Yes, I know." She smiled down at him and Morse's eyelids drooped heavily over his tired eyes. Nessie had said he'd feel a wee bit . . . weary . . .

His head jerked down against his chest, and Fiona settled him against the pillows, gently looking at him as he lay there, and wondering for the dozenth time in her life why all the men who attracted her had either been happily married long, long since, or else were far, far, far too old.

* * *

Morse felt a soft-fingered hand on his right wrist, and opened his eyes to find himself staring up into the face of an extraordinary-looking personage. She was a very small woman, of some seventy-five to eighty summers, wispily white-haired, her face deeply wrinkled and unbeautiful, with an old-fashioned NHS hearing-aid plugged into her left ear, its cord stretching down to a batteried appliance in the pocket of a dirty, loose, grey-woollen cardigan. She appeared näively unaware that any apology might perhaps be called for in wakening a weary patient. Who was she? Who had let her in? It was 9:45 P.M. by the ward clock and two night nurses were on duty. Go away! Go away, you stupid old crow!

"Mr. Horse? Mr. Horse, is it? Her rheumy eyes squinted myopically at the Elastoplast name-tag, and her mouth distended in a dentured smile.

"Morse!" said Morse. "M—O . . ."

"Do you know, I think they've spelt your name wrong, Mr. Horse. I'll try to remember to tell—"

"Morse! M—O—R—S—E!"

"Yes—but it *was* expected, you know. They'd already told me that Wilfrid had only a few days left to live. And we all do get older, don't we? Older every single day."

Yes, yes, clear off! I'm bloody tired, can't you *see*?

"Fifty-two years, we'd been together."

Morse, belatedly, realised who she was, and he nodded more sympathetically now: "Long time!"

"He *liked* being here, you know. He was so grateful to you all—"

"I'm afraid I only came in a couple of days ago—"

"That's exactly why he wanted me to thank *all* of you—all his old friends here." She spoke in a precise, prim manner, with the diction of a retired Latin mistress.

"He was a fine man . . ." began Morse, a little desperately. "I wish I'd got to know him. As I say, though, I only got in a day or two ago—stomach trouble—nothing serious . . ."

The hearing-aid began to whistle shrilly, picking up some internal feedback, and the old lady fiddled about ineffectually with the ear-piece and the control switches. "And that's *why*" (she began now to talk in intermittent italics) "I've got this little *book* for you. He was *so* proud of it. Not that he *said* so, of course—but he *was*. It took him a very long time and it was a *very* happy day for him when it was printed."

Morse nodded with gratitude as she handed him a little booklet in bottle-green paper covers. "It's very kind of you because, as I say, I only came in—"

"Wilfrid would have been *so* pleased."

Oh dear.

"And you will *promise* to read it, won't you?"

"Oh yes—certainly!"

The old lady fingered her whistling aid once more, smiled with the helplessness of a stranded angel, said "Goodbye, Mr. Horse!" and moved on to convey her undying gratitude to the occupant of the adjacent bed.

Morse looked down vaguely at the slim volume thus presented: it could contain no more than—what?—some twenty-odd pages. He would certainly look at it later, as he'd promised. Tomorrow, perhaps. For the moment, he could think of nothing but closing his weary eyes once more, and he placed *Murder on the Oxford Canal*, by Wilfrid M. Deniston, inside his locker, on top of *Scales of Injustice* and *The Blue Ticket*—the triad of new works he'd so recently acquired. Tomorrow, yes . . .

Almost immediately he fell into a deep slumber, where he dreamed of a long cross-country race over the fields of his boyhood, where there, at the distant finishing-line, sat a topless blonde, a silver buckle clasped around her waist, holding in her left hand a pint of beer with a head of winking froth.

Chapter Five

This type of writing sometimes enjoys the Lethean faculty of making those who read it forget to ask what it means, or indeed if it means anything very substantive.
(*Alfred Austin*, The Bridling of Pegasus)

The endoscopy, performed under a mild anaesthetic at 10 A.M. the following morning (Monday), persuaded the surgeons at the JR2 that in Morse's case the knife was probably not needed; their prognosis, too, was modestly encouraging, provided the patient could settle into a more cautiously sober and restrictive regimen for the months (and years) ahead. Furthermore, as a token of their muted optimism, the patient was that very evening to be allowed one half-bowl of oxtail soup and a portion of vanilla ice-cream—and for Morse any gourmand *á la carte* menu could hardly have been more gloriously welcome.

Lewis reported to Sister Maclean at 7:30 P.M., and was unsmilingly nodded through Customs without having to declare one get-well card (from Morse's secretary), a tube of mint-flavoured toothpaste (from Mrs. Lewis), and a clean hand-towel (same provenance). Contentedly, for ten minutes or so, the two men talked of this and that, with Lewis receiving the firm impression that his chief was recovering rapidly.

Fiona the Fair put in a brief appearance towards the end of this visit, shaking out Morse's pillows and placing a jug of cold water on his locker.

"Lovely girl," ventured Lewis.

"You're married—remember?"

"Done any reading yet?" Lewis nodded towards the locker.

"Why do you ask?"

Lewis grinned: "It's the missus—she was just wondering . . ."

"I'm half-way through it, tell her. Riveting stuff!"

"You're not serious—"

"Do you know how to spell 'riveting'?"

"What—one 't' or two, you mean?"

"And do you know what 'stools' are?"

"Things you sit on?"

Morse laughed—a genuine, carefree, pain-free laugh. It was good to have Lewis around; and the vaguely puzzled Lewis was glad to find the invalid in such good spirits.

Suddenly, there beside the bed, re-mitreing the bottom right-hand corner of the blankets, was Sister Maclean herself.

"Who brought the jug of water?" she enquired in her soft but awesome voice.

"It's all right, Sister," began Morse, "the doctor said—"

"Nurse Welch!" The ominously quiet words carried easily across the ward, and Lewis stared at the floor in pained embarrassment as Student Nurse Welch walked warily over to Morse's bed, where she was firmly admonished by her superior. Free access to liquids was to be available only w.e.f. the following dawn—*and not before*. Had the student nurse not read the notes before going the rounds with her water-jugs? And if she had, did she not realise that no hospital could function satisfactorily with such sloppiness? If it mightn't seem important on *this* occasion, did the student nurse not realise that it could be absolutely vital on the *next*?

Another sickening little episode; and for Lewis one still leaving a nasty taste when a few minutes later he bade his chief farewell. Morse himself had said nothing at the time, and said nothing now. Never, he told himself, would he have reprimanded any member of his own staff in such cavalier fashion in

front of other people: and then, sadly, he recalled
that quite frequently he had done precisely that . . .
All the same, he would have welcomed the opportunity of a few quiet words with the duly chastened
Fiona before she went home.

There was virtually no one around in the ward now:
the Ethiopian athlete was doing the hospital rounds
once more; and two of the other patients had shuffled
their way to the gents. Only a woman of about thirty,
a slimly attractive, blonde-headed woman (Walter
Greenaway's daughter, Morse guessed—and guessed
correctly) still sat beside her father. She had given
Morse a quick glance as she'd come in, but now hardly
appeared to notice him as she made her way out of
the ward, and pressed the "Down" button in front of
the top-floor lifts. It was her father who was monopo-
lising her thoughts, and she gave no more than a cursory thought to the man whose name appeared to be
"Morse" and whose eyes, as she had noticed, had followed her figure with a lively interest on her exit.

The time was 8:40 P.M.

Feeling minimally guilty that he had not as yet so
much as opened the cover of the precious work
that Mrs. Lewis had vouchsafed to his keeping,
Morse reached for the book from his locker, and
skimmed through its first paragraph:

Diversity rather than uniformity has almost invariably been seen to characterise the criminal

behaviour-patterns of any technologically developing society. The attempt to resolve any conflicts and or inconsistencies which may arise in the analysis and interpretation of such patterns (see Appendix 3, pp. 492 ff.) is absolutely vital; and the inevitable reinterpretation of this perpetually variable data is the raw material for several recent studies into the causation of criminal behaviour. Yet conflicting strategic choices within heterogeneous areas, starkly differentiated creeds, greater knowledge of variable economic performances, as well as physical, physiological, or physiognomical peculiarities—all these facts (as we shall maintain) can suggest possible avenues never exhaustively explored by any previous student of criminal behaviour in nineteenth-century Britain.

"Christ!" muttered Morse (for the second time that evening). A few years ago he might possibly have considered persevering with such incomprehensible twaddle. But no longer. Stopping momentarily only to marvel at the idiocy of the publisher who had allowed such pompous polysyllaby ever to reach the compositor in the first place, he closed the stout work smartly—and resolved to open it never again.

As it happened, he was to break this instant resolution very shortly; but for the moment there was a rather more attractive proposition awaiting him in his locker: the pornographic paperback which Lewis (praise the Lord!) had smuggled in.

A yellow flash across the glossy cover made its promise to the reader of Scorching Lust and Primitive Sensuality—this claim supported by the picture of a superbly buxom beauty sunning herself on some golden-sanded South-sea island, completely naked except for a string of native beads around her neck. Morse opened the book and skimmed (though a little more slowly than before) a second paragraph that evening. And he was immediately aware of a no-nonsense, clear-cut English style that was going to take the palm every time from the sprawling, spawning, sociological nonsense he had just encountered:

> She surfaced from the pool and began to unbutton her clinging, sodden blouse. And as she did so, the young men all fell silent, urging her—praying her!—in some unheard but deafening chorus, to strip herself quickly and completely—their eyes now rivetted to the carmined tips of her slimly sinuous fingers as they slipped inside her blouse, and so slowly, so tantalisingly, flicked open a further button . . .

"Christ!" It was the third time that Morse had used the same word that evening, and the one that took the prize for blasphemous vehemence. He leaned back against his pillows with a satisfied smile about his lips, clasping to himself the prospect of a couple of hours of delicious titillation on the morrow. He could bend those covers back easily enough; and it would be no great difficulty temporarily to assume the facial expression of a theological student reading some verses from the Minor Prophets. But whatever happened, the chances that Chief Inspector Morse would ever be fully informed about crime and its punishment in nineteenth-century Shropshire had sunk to zero.

For the moment, at any rate.

He replaced *The Blue Ticket* in his locker, on top of *Scales of Injustice*—both books now lying on top of the hitherto neglected *Murder on the Oxford Canal*, that slim volume printed privately under the auspices of The Oxford and County Local History Society.

As Morse nodded off once more, his brain was debating whether there was just the one word misspelled in the brief paragraph he had just read. He would look it up in Chambers when he got home. Lewis hadn't seemed to know, either . . .

Chapter Six

I enjoy convalescence. It is the part that makes the illness worth while.

(*G. B. Shaw*, Back to Methuselah)

At 2 A.M. the inevitable occurred; but fortunately Morse managed to attract the quick attention of the nurse as she'd flitted like some Nightingale around the darkened wards. The noise of the curtains being drawn around his bed sounded to Morse loud enough to rouse the semi-dead. Yet none of his fellow-patients seemed to stir, and she—the blessed girl!—had been quite marvellous.

"I don't even know which way up the thing should go," confided Morse.

"Which way *round*, you mean!" Eileen (such was her name) had whispered, as she proceeded without the slightest embarrassment to explain exactly how the well-trained patient would negotiate

this particular crisis. Then, leaving him with half a
roll of white toilet-paper, and the firm assurance of
a second coming within the next ten minutes, she
was gone.

It was all over—consummated with a bowl of
warm water and a brief squirt of some odoriferous
air-freshener. Whew! Not half as bad as Morse had
feared—thanks to that ethereal girl; and as he
smiled up gratefully at her, he thought there might
have been a look in her eyes that transgressed
the borders of perfunctory nursing. But Morse
would always have thought there was, even if there
wasn't; for he was the sort of man for whom some
area of fantasy was wholly necessary, and his imagination followed the slender Eileen, as elegantly she
walked away: about 5'8'' in height—quite tall
really; in her mid-twenties; eyes greenish-hazel, in a
delicately featured, high-cheekboned face; no ring
of any sort on either hand. She looked so good, so
wholesome, in her white uniform with its dark-blue
trimmings.

Go to sleep, Morse!

At 7:30 A.M., after breakfasting on a single wafer of
Weetabix with an inadequate pour-over of semi-
skimmed milk (and no sugar), Morse noted with
great satisfaction that the NIL BY MOUTH embargo
was now in abeyance, and he poured himself a glass
of water with the joy of a liberated hostage. There

followed for him, that morning, the standard readings of pulse-rate and blood-pressure, a bedside wash in a portable basin, the remaking of his bed, the provision of a fresh jug of water (!), a flirting confab with Fiona, the purchase of *The Times*, a cup of Bovril from the vivacious Violet, and (blessedly) not a single spoke stuck in the hospital machinery from the *éminence grise* installed at the seat of power.

At 10:50 A.M. a white-coated cohort of consultant-cum-underlings came to stand around his bed, and to consider the progress of its incumbent. The senior man, after briefly looking through Morse's file, eyed the patient with a somewhat jaundiced eye.

"How are you feeling this morning?"

"I think I'll live on for a few more weeks—thanks to you," said Morse, with somewhat sickening sycophancy.

"You mention here something about your drinking habits," continued the consultant, unimpressed as it appeared with such spurious gratitude.

"Yes?"

"You drink a lot." It was a statement.

"That's a lot, you think?"

The consultant closed the file with a sigh and handed it back to Nessie. "During my long years in the medical profession, Mr. Morse, I have learned that there are two categories of statistics which can invariably be discounted: the sexual prowess of those suffering from diabetes mellitus; and the boozing habits of our country's middle management."

"I'm not a diabetic."

"You will be if you keep drinking a bottle of Scotch a week."

"Well—perhaps not *every* week."

"You sometimes drink *two* a week, you mean?"

There was a twinkle in the consultant's eye as he waved his posse of acolytes across to the bed of the weakly Greenaway, and sat himself down on Morse's bed.

"Have you had a drop yet?"

"Drop of what?"

"It's a dreadful give-away, you know" (the consultant nodded to the locker) "—that tissue paper."

"Oh!"

"Not *tonight*—all right?"

Morse nodded.

"And one further word of advice. Wait till Sister's off duty!"

"She'd skin me alive!" mumbled Morse.

The consultant looked at Morse strangely. "Well, since you mention it, yes. But that wasn't what I was thinking of, no."

"Something worse?"

"She's about the most forbidding old biddy in the profession; but just remember she comes from north of the border."

"I'm not quite sure . . ."

"She'd probably" (the consultant bent down and whispered in Morse's ear) "—she'd probably draw the curtains and insist on fifty-fifty!"

Morse began to feel more happily settled; and after twenty minutes with *The Times* (Letters read, Crossword completed), one-handedly he folded back the covers of *The Blue Ticket*, and moving comfortably down against his pillows started Chapter One.

"Good book?"

"So-so!" Morse had not been aware of Fiona's presence, and he shrugged non-committally, holding the pages rigidly in his left hand.

"What's it called?"

"Er—*The Blue—The Blue City*."

"Detective story, isn't it? I think my mum's read that."

Morse nodded uneasily. "Do *you* read a lot?"

"I used to, when I was young and beautiful."

"This morning?"

"Sit up!"

Morse leaned forward as she softened up his pillows with a few left hooks and right crosses, and went on her way.

"Lovely girl, isn't she?" It wasn't Lewis this time who made the obvious observation, but the stricken Greenaway, now much recovered, and himself reading a book whose title was plain for all to see: *The Age of Steam*.

Morse pushed his own novel as unobtrusively as possible into his locker: it was a little disappointing, anyway.

"*The Blue Ticket*—that's what it is," said Greenaway.

"Pardon?"

"You got the title wrong—it's *The Blue Ticket*."

"Did I? Ah yes! I, er, I don't know why I'm bothering to read it, really."

"Same reason I did, I suppose. Hoping for a bit of sex every few pages."

Morse grinned defeatedly.

"It's a bit of a let-down," went on Greenaway in his embarrassingly stentorian voice. "My daughter sometimes brings me one or two books like that."

"She was the woman—last night?"

The other nodded. "In library work ever since she was eighteen—twelve years. In the Bodley these last six."

Morse listened patiently to a few well-rehearsed statistics about the mileage of book-shelving in the warrens beneath the Bodleian; and was already learning something of the daughter's *curriculum vitae* when the monologue was terminated by cleaners pushing the beds around in a somewhat cavalier fashion, and slopping their mops into dingily watered buckets.

At 1:30 P.M., after what seemed to him a wretchedly insubstantial lunch, Morse was informed that he was scheduled that afternoon to visit various investigative departments; and that for this purpose the saline-drip would be temporarily removed. And when a hospital porter finally got him comfortably into a wheelchair, Morse felt that he had certainly climbed a rung or two up the convalescence ladder.

It was not until 3:30 P.M. that he returned to the ward, weary, impatient, and thirsty—in reverse order of severity. Roughly, though oddly painlessly, a silent Nessie, just before going off duty, had reaffixed into his right wrist the tube running down from a newly hung drip; and with the eyes of a now fully alert Greenaway upon him, Morse decided that Steve Mingella's sexual fantasies might have to be postponed a while. And when a small, mean-faced Englishwoman (doubtless Violet's understudy) had dispensed just about enough viscous liquid from her tureen to cover the bottom of his soup bowl, Morse's earlier euphoria had almost evaporated. He wouldn't even be seeing Lewis—the latter (as he'd told Morse) taking out the missus for some celebration (reason unspecified). At 7:05 P.M. he managed to sort out his headphones for *The Archers*; and at 7:20 P.M., he decided to dip into the late Colonel's *magnum opus*. By 7:30 P.M.

he was so engrossed that it was only after finishing Part One that he noticed the presence of Christine Greenaway, the beautiful blonde from the Bodley.

Chapter Seven

Murder on the Oxford Canal

The author wishes to acknowledge the help he has so freely received from several sources; but particularly from the Bodleian Library, Oxford; from the *Proceedings of the North Oxford Local History Society*; and from the *Court Registers* of the City of Oxford Assizes, 1859 and 1860.

Further details of the trials mentioned in the following pages may be found in the editions of *Jackson's Oxford Journal* for 20th and 27th August, 1859; and of the same journal for 15th and 22nd April, 1860.

PART ONE
A Profligate Crew

Those who explore the back-streets and the by-ways of our great cities, or indeed our small cities, will sometimes stumble (almost literally, perhaps) upon sad memorials, hidden in neglected churchyards—churchyards which seem wholly separated from any formal ecclesiastical edifice, and which are come across purely by accident at the far side of red-bricked walls, or pressed upon by tall houses—untended, silent, forgotten. Until recent years, such a churchyard was to be found at the lower end of the pretty little road in North Oxford, now designated Middle Way, which links the line of Summertown shops in South Parade with the expensively elegant houses along Squitchey Lane, to the north. But in the early nineteen-sixties most of those tomb-stones which had stood in irregular ranks in the Summertown Parish Churchyard (for such was its official name) were removed from their

original, supracorporal sites in order to afford a
rather less melancholic aspect to those who
were about to pay their deposits on the flats being built upon those highly desirable if slightly
lugubrious acres. Each there in his narrow cell
had once been laid, and each would there remain; yet after 1963 no one, for certain, could
have marked that final resting place.

The few headstones which are adequately
preserved and which are to be found—even to
this day—leaning almost upright against the
northern perimeter of the aforesaid enclave, are
but one tenth or so of the memorials once
erected there, in the second and third quarters
of the nineteenth century, by relatives and
friends whose earnest wish was to perpetuate
the names of those souls, now perhaps known
only to God, who passed their terrestrial lives in
His faith and fear.

One of these headstones, a moss-greened,
limestone slab (standing the furthest away but
three from the present thorough-fare) bears an
epitaph which may still be traced by the prac-
tised eye of the patient epigraphist—though
make haste if you are to decipher that disintegrating lettering!

Beyond this poignant (if unusually lengthy) epitaph there lies a tale of unbridled lust and
drunken lechery; a tale of a hapless and a help-

To the Memory of
JOANNA FRANKS
wife of Charles Franks of London,
who having been primitively and
cruelly assaulted was found most
tragically drowned in the Oxford
Canal on June 22nd 1859,
aged 38 years.
This stone is erected by
some members of the Summertown
Parish Council in commemoration
of the untimely death of this
most unhappy woman.
Lord have mercy upon her soul

Requiescat in Pace Aeterna

less young woman who found herself at the
mercy of coarse and most brutally uninhibited
boatmen, during an horrendous journey made
nearly one hundred and twenty years ago—a journey whose details are the subject-matter of our
present narrative.

Joanna Franks hailed originally from Derby.
Her father, Daniel Carrick, had been accredited
as an agent to the Nottinghamshire and Midlands Friendly Society; and for a good deal of his
married life he appears to have maintained a
position as a reasonably prosperous and well-
respected figure in his home community. Later,
however—and certainly in the few years prior to
the tragic death of his only daughter (there was
a younger brother, Daniel)—he encountered a
period of hard times.

Joanna's first husband was F. T. Donavan,
whose family sprang from County Meath. He is
described by one of his contemporaries as "an
Irishman of many parts," and being a man of
large physique we learn that he was familiarly
(and predictably) known by the nickname of
"Hefty" Donavan. He was a conjurer by profession (or by one of them!) and appeared in many
theatres and music-halls, both in London and in
the provinces. In order to attract some badly
needed publicity, he had at some unspecified
date assumed the splendidly grandiloquent title

of "Emperor of all the Illusionists"; and the following theatre handbill was printed at his own expense to herald his appearance at the City of Nottingham Music Hall in early September 1856:

Mr. Donavan, citizen of the World and of Ireland, most humbly and respectfully informs all members of the upper and the lower nobilities, folk of the landed gentry, and the citizens of the historic district of Nottingham, that in view of his superior and unrivalled excellencies in MAGIC and DECEPTION, he has had conferred upon him, by the supreme conclave of the Assembly of Superior Magicians, this last year, the unchallenged title of EMPEROR of all the Illusionists, and this particularly by virtue of the amazing trick of cutting off a cockerel's head and then restoring the bird to its pristine animation. It was this same DONAVAN, the greatest man in the World, who last week diverted his great audience in Croydon by immersing his whole body, tightly secured and chained, in a tank of the most corrosive acid for eleven minutes and forty-five seconds, as accurately measured by scientific chronometer.

Three years earlier Donavan had written (and found a publisher for) his only legacy to us, a work entitled *The Comprehensive Manual of*

the Conjuring Arts. But the great man's career
was beginning to prove progressively unsuccess-
ful, and no stage appearances whatsoever are
traceable to 1858. In that year, he died, a childless and embittered man, whilst on holiday with
a friend in Ireland, where his grave now rests
in a burial-plot overlooking Bertnaghboy Bay.
Some time afterwards his widow, Joanna, met
and fell deeply in love with one Charles Franks,
an ostler from Liverpool.

Like her first, Joanna's second marriage appears to have been a happy one, in spite of the
fact that times were still hard and money still
scarce. The new Mrs. Franks was to find employment, as a dressmaker and designers' model,
with a Mrs. Russell of 34 Runcorn Terrace, Liverpool. But Franks himself was less successful
in his quest for regular employment, and finally
decided to try his luck in London. Here his great
expectations were soon realised for he was almost immediately engaged as an ostler at the
busy George & Dragon Inn on the Edgware
Road, where we find him duly lodged in the spring
of 1859. In late May of that same year he sent his
wife a guinea (all he could afford) and begged her
to join him in London as soon as possible.

On the morning of Saturday, June 11th, 1859,
Joanna Franks, carrying two small trunks, bade
her farewell to Mrs. Russell in Runcorn Terrace,

and made her way by barge from Liverpool to Preston Brook, the northern terminus of the Trent and Mersey Canal, which had been opened some eighty years earlier. Here she joined one of Pickford & Co.'s express (or "fly") boats[1] which was departing for Stoke-on-Trent and Fradley Junction, and thence, via the Coventry and Oxford Canals, through to London on the main Thames waterway. The fare of sixteen shillings and eleven pence was considerably cheaper than the fare on the Liverpool-London railway line which had been opened some twenty years earlier.

Joanna was an extremely petite and attractive figure, wearing an Oxford-blue dress, with a white kerchief around her neck, and a figured silk bonnet with a bright pink ribbon. The clothes may not have been new; but they were not inexpensive, and they gave to Joanna a very tidy appearance indeed. A very tempting appearance, too, as we shall soon discover.

The captain of the narrow-boat *Barbara Bray* was a certain Jack "Rory" Oldfield from Coventry. According to later testimony of fellow boat-people and other acquaintances, he was basically

---

[1]A "fly" boat travels round the clock, with a double crew, working shifts, with horses exchanged at regular intervals along the canals.

a good-natured sort of fellow, of a blunt, blustery type of address. He was married, though childless, and was aged 42 years. The fellow-members of his crew were: the 30-year-old Alfred Musson, alias Alfred Brotherton, a tall, rather gaunt figure, married with two young children; Walter Towns, alias Walter Thorold, the 26-year-old illiterate son of a farm-labourer, who had left his home town of Banbury in Oxfordshire some ten years earlier; and a teenaged lad, Thomas Wootton, about whom no certain facts have come down to us beyond the probability that his parents came from Ilkeston in Derbyshire.

The *Barbara Bray* left Preston Brook at 7:30 P.M. on Saturday, 11th June. At Fradley Junction, at the southern end of the Mersey Canal, she successfully negotiated her passage through the locks; and at 10 P.M. on Sunday, 19th June, she slipped quietly into the northern reaches of the Coventry Canal, and settled to a course, almost due south, that would lead down to Oxford. Progress had been surprisingly good, and there had been little or no forewarning of the tragic events which lay ahead for the *Barbara Bray*, and for her solitary paying passenger—the small and slimly attractive person of Joanna Franks, for whom such a little span of life remained.

Chapter Eight

> Style is the hallmark of a temperament stamped upon the material at hand.
>
> (*André Maurois*, The Art of Writing)

After reading these few pages, Morse found himself making some mental queries about a few minor items, and harbouring some vague unease about one or two major ones. Being reluctant to disfigure the printed text with a series of marginalia, he wrote a few notes on the back of a daily hospital menu which had been left (mistakenly) on his locker.

The Colonel's style was somewhat on the pretentious side—a bit too high-flown for Morse's taste; and yet the writing was a good deal above the average of its kind—with a pleasing peroration, calculated to ensure in most readers some semi-compulsive page-turning to Part Two. One of the most noticeable characteristics of the writing was the influence of Gray's "Elegy Written in a Country Churchyard"—a poem doubtless stuck down the author's throat as a lad in some minor public school, and one leaving him with a rather lugubrious view of the human lot. One or two *very* nice touches, though, and Morse was prepared to give a couple of ticks to that epithet "supracorporal." He wished, though, he had beside him that most faithful of all his literary companions, *Chambers' English Dictionary,* for although he had frequently met "ostler" in crossword puzzles, he wasn't sure *exactly* what an ostler did; and "figured" bonnet wasn't all that obvious, was it?

Thinking of writing—and writing books—old Donavan (Joanna's first) must have been pretty competent. After all, he'd "found a publisher" for his great work. And until the last few years of his life, this literate Irish conjurer was seemingly pulling in the crowds at all points between Croydon and Burton-on-Trent . . . He must certainly have had *something* about him, this man of many parts. "Greatest man in the World" might be going over the top a bit, yet a mild degree of megalomania was perhaps forgivable in the publicity material of such a multi-talented performer?

"Bertnaghboy Bay?"—Morse wrote on the menu. His knowledge of geography was minimal. At his junior school, his teachers had given him a few assorted facts about the exports of Argentina, Bolivia, Chile, and the rest; and at the age of eight he had known—and still knew (with the exception of South Dakota)—all the capital cities of the American States. But that was the end of his apprenticeship in that discipline. After winning a scholarship to the local grammar school, the choice of the three "G"s had been thrust upon him: Greek, German, or Geography. Little real choice, though, for he had been thrust willy-nilly into the Greek set, where the paradigms of nouns and verbs precluded any knowledge of the Irish counties. Where *was*—what was the name?—Bertnaghboy Bay?

It was paradoxical, perhaps, that Morse should have suddenly found himself so fascinated by the Oxford Canal. He was aware that many people were besotted with boat-life, and he deemed it wholly proper that parents should seek to hand on to their offspring some love of sailing, or rambling, or keeping pets, or bird-watching, or whatever. But in Morse's extremely limited experience, narrow-boating figured as a grossly over-rated activity. Once, on the invitation of a pleasant enough couple, he had agreed to be piloted from the terminus of the Oxford Canal at Hythe Bridge Street up to the Plough at Wolvercote—a journey of only a couple of miles, which would be accomplished (he was assured) within the hour; but which in fact had been so fraught with manifold misfortunes that the finishing line was finally reached with only five

minutes' drinking-time remaining—and that on a
hot and thirsty Sunday noon. That particular boat
had required a couple of people—one to steer the
thing and one to keep hopping out for locks and
what the handbook called "attractive little draw-
bridges." Now, Joanna's boat had got four of them
on it—five with her; so it must surely have been aw-
fully crowded on that long and tedious journey,
pulled slowly along by some unenthusiastic horse.
Too long! Morse nodded to himself—he was beginning to get the picture . . . Far quicker by rail, of
course! And the fare she'd paid, 16s 11d, seemed on
the face of it somewhat on the steep side for a trip
as a passenger on a working-boat. In 1859? Surely
so! What would the rail-fare have been then?
Morse had no idea. But there were ways of finding
out; there were people who knew these things . . .

He could still see in his mind's eye the painting
on the cabin in which he'd travelled, with its lake,
its castle, its sailing boat, and range of mountains—
all in the traditional colours of red, yellow, green.
But what was it like to *live* in such boats? Boats that
in the nineteenth century had been crewed by as-
sortments of men from all over the place: from the
Black Country; from the colliery villages around
Coventry and Derby and Nottingham; from the
terraced cottages in Upper Fisher Row by the terminus in Oxford—carrying their cargoes of coal,
salt, china, agricultural produce . . . other things.

What other things? And why on earth all those "aliases"? Were the crewmen counted a load of crooks before they ever came to court? Did every one on the Canal have two names—a "bye-name," as it were, as well as one written in the christening-book? Surely any jury was bound to feel a fraction of prejudice against such ... such ... even before ... He was feeling tired, and already his head had jerked up twice after edging by degrees towards his chest.

Charge Nurse Eileen Stanton had come on duty at 9 P.M., and Morse was still sound asleep at 9:45 P.M. when she went quietly to his bedside and gently took the hospital menu from his hand and placed it on his locker. He was probably dreaming, she decided, of some *haute cuisine* from Les Quat' Saisons, but she would have to wake him up very shortly, for his evening pills.

Chapter Nine

> What a convenient and delightful world is this world of books—if you bring to it not the obligations of the student, or look upon it as an opiate for idleness, but enter it rather with the enthusiasm of the adventurer.
> (*David Grayson*, Adventures in Contentment)

The following morning (Wednesday) was busy and blessed. Violet's early offerings of bran flakes, semi-burnt cold toast, and semi-warm weak tea, were wonderfully welcome; and when at 10 A.M. Fiona had come to remove the saline-drip (permanently), Morse knew that the gods were smiling. When, further, he walked down the corridor now to the wash-room, without encumbrance, and without attendant, he felt like Florestan newly released from confinement in Act 2 of *Fidelio*. And when with full movement of both arms he freely soaped his hands and face, and examined the rather sorry job he'd earlier made of shaving, he felt a wonderfully happy man.

Once out of this place (he decided) he would make
some suitable, not too startling, donation to the staff
in general, and invite, in particular, his favourite
nurse (odds pretty even for the moment between
the Fair and the Ethereal) to that restaurant in
North Oxford where he would show off his (limited) knowledge of modern Greek and order a
Mezéthes Tavérnas menu, the one billed as "an epi-
curean feast from first dip to final sweet." Ten quid
per person, or a little more; and with wine—and
liqueurs, perhaps—and one or two little extras, £30
should cover it, he hoped ... Not that the creamy-
skinned Eileen would be on duty that night. Some
domestic commitments, she'd said. "Domestic?" It
worried Morse, just a little. Still, so long as Nessie
wasn't going to be prowling around ... because
Morse had decided that, in the interests of his convalescence, he might well twist the little bottle's golden
cap that very night.

Back in the ward, the time passed, one could say,
satisfactorily. A cup of Bovril at 10:30 A.M. was followed by a further recital from Mr. Greenaway
of his daughter's quite exceptional qualities—a
woman without whom, it appeared, the Bodleian
would have considerable difficulty in discharging
any of its academic functions. After which, Morse
was visited by one of the ten-a-penny dietitians in
the place—a plain-looking, serious-souled young
madam, who took him *seriatim* through a host of

low-calorie vegetables on which he could "fill up" *ad libitum*: asparagus; bamboo-shoots; beans (broad); beans (French); beans (runner); bean-sprouts; broccoli; Brussels sprouts; cabbage (various); cauliflower; celery; chicory; chives; courgettes; cucumber—and that was only the first three letters in the eternal alphabet of a healthy dietary. Morse was so impressed with the recital of the miraculous opportunities which awaited him that he even fore-bore to comment on the assertion that both tomato-juice and turnip-juice were wonderfully tasty and nutritious alternatives to alcoholic beverages. Dutifully, he sought to nod at suitable intervals, knowing deep down that he could, should, and bloody well *would*, shed a couple of stone fairly soon. Indeed, as an earnest of his new-found resolution, he insisted on only one scoop of potatoes, and no thickened gravy whatsover, when Violet brought her lunch-time victuals round.

In the early afternoon, after listening to the repeat of *The Archers*, the most pleasing thought struck him: no work that day at Police HQ; no worries about an evening meal; no anxieties for the morrow, except perhaps those occasioned by his newly awakened consciousness of infirmity—and of death. But not that even *that* worried him too much, as he'd confessed to Lewis: no next of kin, no dependants, no need for looking beyond a purely selfish gratification. And Morse knew exactly what he wanted now, as he sat upright, clean, cool, relaxed, against the pillows. Because, strange as it may seem, for the present he wouldn't have given two Madagascan monkeys for a further couple of chapters of *The Blue Ticket*. At that moment, and most strongly, he felt the enthusiasm of the voyager—the voyager along the canal from Coventry to Oxford. Happily, therefore, he turned to *Murder on the Oxford Canal*, Part Two.

Chapter Ten

PART TWO
A Proven Crime

Although at the time there were a few conflicting statements about individual circumstances in the following, and fatal, sequence of events, the general pattern as presented here is—and, indeed, always has been—undisputed.

The 38-odd mile stretch of the Coventry Canal (of more interest today to the industrial archaeologist than to the lover of rural quietude) appears to have been negotiated without any untoward incident, with recorded stops at the Three Tuns Inn at Fazely, and again at the Atherstone Locks, further south. What can be asserted with well-nigh certitude is that the *Barbara Bray* reached Hawkesbury Junction, at the northern end of Oxford Canal, an hour or so

before midnight on Monday, 20th June. Today,
the distance from Hawkesbury Junction down to
Oxford is some 77 miles; and in 1859 the journey
was very little longer. We may therefore assume
that even with one or two protracted stops along
the route, the double crew of the "fly" boat *Barbara Bray* should have managed the journey
within about thirty-six hours. And this appears
to have been the case. What now follows is a reconstruction of those crucial hours, based both
upon the evidence given at the subsequent trials
(for there were two of them) and upon later research, undertaken by the present author and
others, into the records of the Oxford Canal
Company Registers and the Pickford & Co.
Archives. From all the available evidence, one
saddening fact stands out, quite stark and incontrovertible: the body of Joanna Franks was found
just after 5:30 A.M. on Wednesday, 22nd June, in
the Oxford Canal—in the triangular-shaped
basin of water known as "Duke's Cut," a short
passage through to the River Thames dug by the
fourth Duke of Marlborough in 1796, about two
and a half miles north of the (then) canal terminus at Hayfield Wharf in the city of Oxford.

For the moment, however, let us make a jump
forward in time. After a Coroner's inquest at the
Running Horses Inn (now demolished, but formerly standing on the corner of Upper Fisher

Row by Hythe Bridge in Oxford) the four crew members of the *Barbara Bray* were straightly charged with the murder of Joanna Franks, and were duly committed to the nearby Oxford Gaol. In the preliminary trial, held at the Oxford Summer Assizes of August 1859, there were three indictments against these men: the wilful murder of Joanna Franks by throwing her into the canal; rape upon the said woman, with different counts charging different prisoners with being principals in the commission of the offence and the others as aiders and abettors; and the stealing of various articles, the property of her husband. To a man, the crew pleaded not guilty to all charges. (Wootton, the boy, who was originally charged with them, was not named in the final indictments.)

Mr. Sergeant Williams, for the prosecution, said he should first proceed on the charge of rape. However, after the completion of his case, the Judge (Mr. Justice Traherne) decided that there could be no certain proof of the prisoners having committed the crime, and the Jury was therefore directed to return a verdict of "Not Guilty" on that charge. Mr. Williams then applied to the Court for a postponement of the trial under the indictment for murder, until the next Assizes, on the grounds that a material witness, Joseph Jarnell, formerly a co-prisoner in Oxford

Gaol, and previously committed for bigamy, could not be heard before the Court until he had obtained a free pardon from the Secretary of State. Oldfield, the boat's captain, was understood to have made some most important disclosure to Jarnell while the two men shared the same prison-cell. Although this request was strenuously opposed by Oldfield's Counsel, Mr. Judge Traherne finally consented to the suggested postponement.

The Judge appointed for the second trial, held in April 1860, was Mr. Augustus Benham. There was intense public feeling locally, and the streets leading to the Assizes Court in Oxford were lined with hostile crowds. The case had also excited considerable interest among many members of the legal profession. The three prisoners appeared at the bar wearing the leather belts and sleeve waistcoats usually worn at that time by the canal boatmen, and were duly charged with "wilful murder, by casting, pushing, and throwing the said Joanna Franks into the Oxford Canal by which means she was choked, suffocated, and drowned." What exactly, we must ask, had taken place on those last few, fatal miles above the stretch of water known as Duke's Cut on the Oxford Canal? The tragic story soon began to unfold itself.

There are more than adequate grounds for

believing that the journey from Preston Brook down to the top of the Oxford Canal at Hawkesbury was comparatively uneventful, although it soon became known that Oldfield had sat with Joanna in the cabin while the boat was negotiated through the Northwich and Harecastle Tunnels. However, from the time the *Barbara Bray* reached the lonely locks of Napton Junction— 30-odd miles down from Hawkesbury, and with Oxford still some 50 miles distant—the story appears to change, and to change (as we shall see) dramatically.

William Stevens, a canal clerk employed by Pickford & Co., confirmed[1] that the *Barbara Bray* reached the Napton Locks at about 11 A.M. on Tuesday 21st June, and that the boat remained there, in all, for about an hour and a half. "There was a woman passenger on board," and she complained immediately to Stevens about "the conduct of the men with whom she was driven to associate." It would, he agreed, have been proper for him to have logged the complaint (the *Barbara Bray* was, after all, a Pickford & Co. transport); but he had not done so, confining his advice to the suggestion that the woman should

---

[1]Many of the facts in the account used here are taken from the *Court Registers* of the Oxford Assizes, 1860, and from the *verbatim* transcript of those parts of the trial reported in *Jackson's Oxford Journal*, April 1860 (passim).

report forthwith to the Company offices in Oxford, where it should be possible for her to
switch to another boat on the last leg of her
journey. Stevens had witnessed some shouted
altercations between Joanna and a member of
the crew, and remembered hearing Joanna
speak the words: "Leave me alone—I'll have
nothing to do with you!" Two of the men (Oldfield and Musson, he thought) had used some utterly disgraceful language, although he agreed
with Counsel for the defence that the language of almost all boatmen at these times was
equally deplorable. What seemed quite obvious
to Stevens was that the crew were beginning to
get very much the worse for drink, and he gave it
as his opinion that they were "making very free
with the spirit which was the cargo." Before setting off, the woman had complained yet again
about the behaviour of the men, and Stevens
had repeated his advice to her to reconsider her
position once the boat reached the terminus of
the Oxford Canal—where a partial off-loading
of the cargo was officially scheduled.

It appears, in fact, that Stevens's advice did
not go unheeded. At Banbury, some twelve miles
further down the canal, Joanna made a determined effort to seek alternative transport for
the remainder of her journey. Matthew Laurenson, wharfinger at Tooley's Yard, remembered

most clearly Joanna's "urgent enquiries" about the times of "immediate coaches to London— and coaches from Oxford to Banbury." But nothing was convenient, and again Joanna was advised to wait until she got to Oxford—now only some 20 miles away. Laurenson put the time of this meeting as approximately 6:30-7 P.M. (it is hardly surprising that times do not always coincide exactly in the court evidence—let us recall that we are almost ten months after the actual murder), and was able to give as his general impression of the unfortunate woman that she was "somewhat flushed and afeared."

As it happened, Joanna was now to have a fellow passenger, at least for a brief period, since Agnes Laurenson, the wharfinger's wife, herself travelled south on the *Barbara Bray* down to King's Sutton Lock (five miles distant); she, too, was called to give evidence at the trial. Recalling that there was "a fellow passenger aboard who looked very agitated," Mrs. Laurenson stated that Joanna may have had a drink, but that she seemed completely sober, as far as could be judged—unlike Oldfield and Musson—and that she was clearly most concerned about her personal safety.

The tale now gathers apace towards its tragic conclusion; and it was the landlord of The Crown & Castle at Aynho (just below Banbury) who was able to provide some of the most telling and damning testimony of all. When Mrs. Laurenson had left the boat three miles upstream at King's Sutton, it would appear that Joanna could trust herself with the drunken boatmen no longer, according to the landlord, who had encountered her at about 10 P.M. that night. She had arrived, on foot, a little earlier and confessed that she was so frightened of the lecherous drunkards on the *Barbara Bray* that she had determined to walk along the tow-path, even at that late hour, and to take her chances with the considerably lesser evils of foot-pads and cut-purses. She hoped (she'd said) that it would be safely possible for her to rejoin the boat later when its crew might be a few degrees the more sober. Whilst she waited for the boat to come up, the landlord offered her a glass of stout, but Joanna declined. He had kept an eye on her, however, and noticed that as she sat by the edge of the canal she appeared to be secretly sharpening a knife on the side of the lock (Musson was later found to have a cut on his left cheek, and this could have been, and probably was, made with the same knife). As the boat had drawn alongside Aynho wharf, one of the crew (the landlord was unable to say which) had "cursed the eyes of the woman and wished her in hell flames, for he loathed and detested the very sight of her." As she finally reboarded the boat, the landlord remembered seeing Joanna being offered a drink; and, in fact, he thought she might have taken a glass. But this evidence must be discounted wholly, since Mr. Bartholomew Samuels, the Oxford surgeon who conducted an immediate *postmortem*, found no evidence whatsoever of any alcohol in poor Joanna's body.

George Bloxham, the captain of a northwardbound Pickford boat, testified that he had drawn alongside Oldfield's boat just below Aynho, and that a few exchanges had been made, as normal, between the two crews. Oldfield had referred to his woman passenger in terms which were completely "disgusting," vowing, in the crudest language, what he would do with her that very night "or else he would burke her."[2] Bloxham added that Oldfield was very drunk; and Musson and Towns, too, were "rather well away, the pair of 'em."

James Robson, keeper of the Somerton Deep Lock, said that he and his wife, Anna, were awakened at about midnight by a scream of terror coming from the direction of the lock. At first they had assumed it was the cry of a young child; but when they looked down from the bedroom

[2]Burke was a criminal who had been executed some thirty years earlier for smothering his victims and then selling their bodies for medical dissection.

window of the lock-house, they saw only some men by the side of the boat, and a woman seated on top of the cabin with her legs hanging down over the side. Three things the Robsons were able to recall from that grim night, their evidence proving so crucial at the trial. Joanna had called out in a terrified voice "I'll not go down! Don't attempt me!" Then one of the crew had shouted "Mind her legs! Mind her legs!"

And after that the passenger had resumed her frightened screams: "What have you done with my shoes—oh! please tell me!" Anna Robson enquired who the woman was, and was told by one of the crew: "A passenger—don't worry!", the crewman adding that she was having words with her husband, who was with her aboard.

Forbidding to Joanna as the tall lock-house must have appeared that midnight, standing sentinel-like above the black waters, it presented her with her one last chance of life—had she sought asylum within its walls.

But she made no such request.

At this point, or shortly after, it appears that the terrified woman took another walk along the tow-path to escape the drunken crew; but she was almost certainly back on board when the boat negotiated Gibraltar Lock. After which—and only some very short time after—she must have been out walking (yet again!) since Robert

Bond, a crew-hand from the narrow-boat *Isis*, gave evidence that he passed her on the tow-path. Bond recorded his surprise that such an attractive woman should be out walking on her own so late, and he recalled asking her if all was well. But she had only nodded, hurriedly, and passed on into the night. As he approached Gibraltar Lock, Bond had met Oldfield's boat, and was asked by one of its crew if he had seen a woman walking the tow-path, the man adding, in the crudest terms, what he would do to her once he had her in his clutches once again.

No one, apart from the evil boatmen on the *Barbara Bray*, was ever to see Joanna Franks alive again.

Chapter Eleven

> 'Pon my word, Watson, you are coming along won-
> derfully. You have really done very well indeed. It is
> true that you have missed everything of importance,
> but you have hit upon the method.
>
> (*Sir Arthur Conan Doyle*, A Case of Identity)

As with Part One, Morse found himself making a
few notes (mentally, this time) as he read through
the unhappy narrative. For some reason he felt
vaguely dissatisfied with himself. Something was
nagging at his brain about Part One; but for the
present he was unable to put a finger on it. It would
come back to him once he'd re-read a few pages.
No hurry, was there? None. The theoretical problem which his mind had suddenly seized upon was
no more than a bit of harmless, quite inconsequential amusement. And yet the doubts persisted in his
brain: could anyone, *anyone*, read this story and not
find himself questioning one or two of the points so

confidently reported? Or two or three of them? Or three or four?

What was the normal pattern of entertainment for canal boatmen, like Oldfield, on those "protracted stops" of theirs? Changing horses was obviously one of the key activities on such occasions, but one scarcely calculated to gladden every soul. Dropping in at the local knocking-shop, then? A likely port-of-call for a few of the more strongly sexed among them, most surely. And drink? Did they drink their wages away, these boatmen, in the low-beamed bars that were built along their way? How not? Why not? What else was there to do? And though drink (as the Porter once claimed) might take away the performance, who could gainsay that it frequently provoked the desire? The desire, in this case, to rape a beautiful woman-passenger.

So many questions.

But if sex was at the bottom of things, why were the rape charges dropped at the first trial? Agreed, there was no DNA biological fingerprinting in the 1850s; no genetic code that could be read into some desperate fellow's swift ejaculations. But even in that era, the charge of rape could often be made to stick without too much difficulty; and Confucius's old pleasantry about the comparative immobility of a man with his trousers round his ankles must have sounded just as hollow then as now. Certainly to the ears of Joanna Franks.

The footnote referring to the *Court Registers* had been a surprise, and it would be of interest, certainly to the sociologist, to read something of contemporary attitudes to rape in 1859. Pretty certainly it would be a few leagues less sympathetic than that reflected in Morse's morning copy of *The Times*: "Legal Precedent in Civil Action—£35,000 Damages for Rape Victim." Where were those Registers, though—if they still existed? They might (Morse supposed) have explained the Colonel's bracketed caveat about discrepancies. But *what* discrepancies? There must have been *something* in old Deniston's mind, something that bothered him just that tiny bit. The Greeks had a word for it—*parakrousis*—the striking of a slightly wrong note in an otherwise tuneful harmony.

Was that "wrong note" struck by Mrs. Laurenson, perhaps? Whatever the situation had been with Joanna, this Laurenson woman (with her husband's full assent, one must assume) had joined the *Barbara Bray* for the journey down to King's Sutton with—as the reader was led to believe—a boatload of sexually rampant dipsomaniacs. Difficult to swallow? Unless of course the wharfinger, Laurenson, was perfectly happy to get rid of his missus for the night—or for any night. But such a line of reasoning seemed fanciful, and there was a further possibility—a very simple, and really rather a startling one: that the crew of the *Barbara Bray* had *not* been all that belligerently blotto at the time! But no. Every piece of evidence—surely!—pointed in the opposite direction; pointed to the fact that the boatmen's robes of honour (in Fitzgeraldian phrase) were resting, like the Confucian rapist's, only just above their bootlaces.

Boots . . . shoes . . .

What *was* all that about those shoes? Why were they figuring so prominently in the story? There would surely have been more intimate items of Joanna's wardrobe to pilfer if the crewmen had been seeking to effect some easier sexual congress. One of them *might*, perhaps, have been a clandestine foot-fetishist . . .

Morse, telling himself not to be so stupid, looked again at the last couple of pages of the text. A bit over-written, all that stuff about the sentinel-like old lock-house, looking out over the dark waters. Not bad, though: and at least it made Morse resolve to drive out and see it for himself, once he was well again. Unless the planners and the developers had already pulled it down.

Like they'd pulled down St. Ebbe's . . .

Such were some of Morse's thoughts after reading his second instalment. It was quite natural that he should wish to eke out the pleasures afforded by the Colonel's test. Yet it must be admitted that, once again, Morse had almost totally failed to conceive the real problems raised by this narrative. Usually, Morse was a league and a league in front of any competitive intellects; and even now his thought processes were clear and unorthodox. But for the time being, he was far below his best. Too near the picture. He was standing where the coloured paints on the narrow-boat's sides had little chance of imposing any pattern on his eye. What he really needed was to stand that bit further back from the picture; to get a more synoptic view of things. "Synoptic" had always been one of Morse's favourite words. Quickly Morse re-read Part Two. But he seemed to see little more in general terms than he had done earlier, although there were a few extra points of detail which had evaded him on the first reading, and he stored them away, haphazardly, in his brain.

There was that capital "J," for example, that the Colonel favoured whenever he wished to emphasise the enormity of human iniquity and the infallibility of Jury and Judicature—like the capital "G" the Christian churches always used for God.

Then there were those journeys through the two tunnels, when Oldfield had sat with Joanna . . . or when, as Morse translated things, he put his arm around the frightened girl in the eerie darkness, and told her not to be afraid . . .

And those last complex, confusing paragraphs! She had been desperately anxious to get off the boat and away from her tipsy persecutors—so much seemed beyond any reasonable doubt. But, if so, why, according to that self-same evidence, had she always been so anxious to get back *on* again?

Airy-fairy speculation, all this; but there were at least two things that could be factually checked. "Nothing was convenient," it had said, and any researcher worth his salt could easily verify *that*. What *was* available, at the time Joanna reached Banbury? He could also soon discover how much any alternative route to London would have cost. What, for example, was the rail-fare to London in 1859? For that matter, what exactly had been the rail-fare between *Liverpool* and London, a fare which appeared to have been beyond the Franks's joint financial resources?

Interesting . . .

As, come to think of it, were those double quotation-marks in the text—presumably the actual words, directly transcribed, and reported *verbatim*, and therefore primary source-material for the crewmen's trial. Morse looked through the interspersed quotations again, and one in particular caused his mind to linger: "coaches to London—and coaches from Oxford to Banbury." Now, if those were the *exact* words Joanna had used . . . *if* they were . . . Why had she asked for the times of coaches "from Oxford to Banbury"? Surely, she should have been asking about coaches *from Banbury to Oxford*. Unless . . . unless . . .

Again, it all seemed most interesting—at least to Morse. What, finally, was he to make of that drink business? Had Joanna been drinking—or had she not? There was some curious ambivalence in the text; and perhaps this may have been in the Colonel's mind when he referred to "a few conflicting statements"? But no—that was impossible. Mr. Bartholomew Samuels had found no alcohol in Joanna's body, and that was that!

Or, rather, would have been, to most men.

The thought of drink had begun to concentrate Morse's mind powerfully, and with great circumspection and care, Morse poured a finger of Scotch into his bedside glass, with the same amount of plain water. Wonderful! Pity that no one would ever believe his protestations that Scotch was a necessary stimulant to his brain cells! For after a few minutes his mind was flooding with ideas—exciting ideas!—and furthermore he realised that he could begin to test one or two of his hypotheses that very evening.

That is, if Walter Greenaway's daughter came to visit.

Chapter Twelve

Th' first thing to have in a libry is a shelf. Fr'm time to time this can be decorated with lithrachure. But th' shelf is th' main thing.

(*Finley Peter Dunne*, Mr. Dooley Says)

As she walked down Broad Street at 7:40 A.M. the following morning (Thursday), Christine Green-away was thinking (*still* thinking) about the man who had spoken to her the previous evening in Ward 7C on the top floor of the JR2. (It was only on rare occasions that she welcomed her father's pride in his ever-loving daughter!) It wasn't that she'd been obsessively preoccupied with the man ever since; but there had been a semi-waking, overnight awareness of him. All because he'd asked her, so nicely, to look up something for him in the Bodley. So earnest, so grateful, he'd seemed. And that was silly, really, because she'd willingly have helped

him, anyway. That's why she'd become a librarian
in the first place: to be able to locate some of the
landmarks in the fields of History and Literature,
and to provide where she could the correct map-
references for so many curious enquiries. Even as a
five-year-old, with her blonde plaits reaching half-
way down her bony back, she'd envied the woman
in the Summertown Library who similarly located
tickets somewhere in the long drawers behind the
high counter; envied, even more, the woman who
stamped the dates in the front of the borrowed
books, and inserted each little ticket into its appropriate, oblong folder. Not that she, Christine
Greenaway, performed any longer such menial
tasks herself. Almost forgotten now were those inevitable queries of who wrote *The Wind in the Wil-
lows*; for she, Christine, was now the senior of the
three august librarians who sat at the northern end
of the Bodleian's Lower Reading Room, where her
daily duties demanded assistance to both senior
and junior members of the University: checking
slips, identifying shelf-marks, suggesting reference-
sections, making and taking phone-calls (one,
yesterday, from the University of Uppsala). And
over these last years she had felt a sense of importance and enjoyment in her job—of functioning
happily in the workings of the University.

Of course, there had been some major disappointments in her life, as there had been, she knew,

with most folk. Married at twenty-two, she had
been a divorcée at twenty-three. No other woman
on his part; no other man on hers—although there'd
been (still were) so many opportunities. No! It
was simply that her husband had been so immature
and irresponsible—and, above all, so boring! Once
the pair of them had got down to running a
home, keeping a monthly budget, checking bank-
statements—well, she'd known he could never
really be the man for her. And as things now stood,
she could no longer stomach the prospect of another
mildly ignorant, semi-aggressively macho figure of
a bed-mate. Free as she was of any financial worries, she could do exactly as she wished about issues
that were important to *her*; and she had become a
modestly active member of several organisations,
including Greenpeace, CND, the Ramblers' Association, and the RSPB. Quite certainly, she would
never join one of those match-making societies
with the hope of finding a more interesting specimen than her former spouse. If ever she *did* look
for another husband, he would have to be someone
she could, in some way, come to *respect*: to respect
for his conversation or his experience or his intel-
lect or his knowledge or his—well, his anything at
all, really, except a pride in his sexual prowess. So
what (she asked herself) had all this got to do with
him? Not much to look at, was he? Balding, and
quite certainly carrying considerable excess weight

around the midriff. Though, to be honest with herself, she was beginning to feel a grudging regard for those men who were just *slightly* overweight, perhaps because she herself seemed never able to put on a few pounds—however much she overindulged in full-cream cakes and deep-fried fish and chips.

Forget him! Forget him, Christine!

Such self-admonition prevailed as she walked that morning down the Broad, past Balliol and Trinity on her left, before crossing over the road, just before Blackwell's, and proceeding, *sub imperatoribus*, up the semi-circular steps into the gravelled courtyard of the Sheldonian. Thence, keeping to her right, she walked past the SILENCE PLEASE notice under the archway, and came out at last into her real home territory—the Quadrangle of the Schools.

For many days, when six years earlier she had first started working at the Bodleian, she had been conscious of the beautiful setting there. Over the months and years, though, she had gradually grown over-familiar with what the postcards on sale in the Proscholium still called "The Golden Heart of Oxford"; grown familiar, as she'd regularly trodden the gravelled quad, with the Tower of the Five Orders to her left, made her way past the bronze statue of the third Earl of Pembroke, and entered the Bodleian Library through the great single doorway in the west side, beneath the four tiers of blind arches in their gloriously mellowed stone.

Different today though—so very different! She felt once again the sharp irregularities of the gravel-stones beneath the soles of her expensive, high-heeled, leather shoes. And she was happily aware once more of the mediaeval Faculties painted over those familiar doors around the quad. In particular, she looked again at her favourite sign: SCHOLA NATURALIS PHILOSOPHIAE, the gilt capital-letters set off, with their maroon border, against a background of the deepest Oxford-blue. And as she climbed the wooden staircase to the Lower Reading Room, Christine Greenaway reminded herself, with a shy smile around her thinly delicious lips, why perhaps it had taken her so long to re-appreciate those neglected delights that were all around her.

She hung her coat in the Librarians' Cloakroom, and started her daily duties. It was always tedious, that first hour (7:45–8:45 A.M.), clearing up the books left on the tables from the previous day, and ensuring that the new day's readers could be justifiably confident that the Bodley's books once more stood ready on their appointed shelves.

She thought back to the brief passages of conversation the previous evening, when he'd nodded over to her (only some six feet away):

"You work at the Bodleian, I hear?"

"Uh-huh!"

"It may be—it is!—a bit of a cheek, not knowing you . . ."

"—but you'd like me to look something up for you."

Morse nodded, with a winsome smile.

She'd known he was some sort of policeman—things like that always got round the wards pretty quickly. His eyes had held hers for a few seconds, but she had been conscious neither of their blueness nor of their authority: only their melancholy and their vulnerability. Yet she had sensed that those complicated eyes of his had seemed to look, somehow, deep down inside herself, and *to like what they had seen*.

"Silly twerp, you are!" she told herself. She was behaving like some adolescent schoolgirl, smitten with a sudden passion for a teacher. But the truth remained—that for that moment she was prepared to run a marathon in clogs and calipers for the whitish-haired and gaudily pyjamaed occupant of the bed immediately opposite her father's.

Chapter Thirteen

Ah, fill the Cup:—what boots it to repeat
How Time is slipping underneath our Feet:
Unborn To-morrow, and dead Yesterday,
Why fret about them if To-day be sweet!
                    (*Edward Fitzgerald*,
          The Rubaiyat of Omar Khayyam)

He'd been rather vague, and it had been somewhat difficult precisely to assess what he wanted: some specific details about any assurance or insurance companies in the mid-nineteenth century—especially, if it were possible, about companies in the Midlands. Off and on, during the morning, it had taken her an hour or more to hunt down the appropriate catalogues; and another hour to locate the pertinent literature. But by lunchtime (praise be!) she had completed her research, experiencing, as she assumed, an elation similar to that of the scholars who daily dug into the treasury of her Great Library to extract their small nuggets of gold. She had found a work of reference which told her exactly what Morse (the man responsible for ruffling her wonted calm) had wanted her to find.

Just after twelve noon, with one of her female colleagues, she walked over to the King's Arms, on the corner of Holywell Street—in which hostelry she was accustomed to enjoy her fifty-five-minute lunch-break, with a single glass of white wine and a salmon-and-cucumber sandwich. It was when Christine got to her feet and offered to get in a second round of drinks, that her colleague eyed her curiously.

"You always said two glasses sent you to sleep."

"So?"

"So I'll go to sleep as well, all right?"

They were good friends; and doubtless Christine would have given some castrated account of her visit to the JR2 the previous evening, had not another colleague joined them. Whereafter the three were soon engaged in happily animated conversation about interior decorating and the iniquity of current mortgage-repayments.

Or two of them were, to be more accurate. And the one who had been the least lively of the trio found herself doing rather less work than usual that same afternoon. After carefully photocopying her finds, she wished the P.M. hours away, for she was impatient to parade the fruits of her research;

and she just, simply—well, she just wanted to see the man again. That was all.

At 6:30 P.M. at her home in the village of Bletchington, some few miles out of Oxford, towards Otmoor, she slowly stroked red polish on to her smoothly manicured oval nails, and at 7 P.M. started out for the JR2.

Equally, from his own vantage point, Morse was looking forward to seeing Christine Greenaway once again. The previous evening he'd quickly appreciated her professionalism as she'd listened to his request, as she'd calculated how it might be implemented. In a more personal way he'd noted, too, the candour and intelligence of her eyes—eyes almost as blue as his own—and the quiet determination around her small mouth. So it was that at 7:25 P.M. he was sitting in his neatly re-made bed, newly washed, erect against his pillows, his thinning hair so recently re-combed—when his stomach suddenly felt as though it was being put through a mangle; and for two or three minutes the pain refused to relax its grinding, agonising grip. Morse closed his eyes and squeezed his fists with such force that the sweat stood out on his forehead; and with eyes still shut he prayed to Someone, in spite of his recent conversion from agnosticism to outright atheism.

Two years earlier, at the Oxford Book Association, he had listened to a mournful Muggeridge propounding the disturbing philosophy of The Fearful Symmetry, in which the debits and the credits on the ledgers are balanced inexorably and eternally, and where the man who tries to steal a secret pleasure will pretty soon find himself queuing up to pay the bill—and more often than not with some hefty service-charges added in. What a preposterous belief it was (the sage had asserted) that the hedonist could be a happy man!

Oh dear!

Why had Morse ever considered the pleasure of a little glass? The wages of sin was death, and the night before was seldom worth the morning after (some people said). All mortals, Morse knew, were ever treading that narrow way by Tophet flare to Judgement Day, but he now prayed that the last few steps in his own case might be deferred at least a week or two.

Then, suddenly as it had come, the pain was gone, and Morse opened his eyes once more.

The clock behind Sister's desk (as earlier and darkly rumoured, Nessie was going to be on the night-shift) was showing 7:30 when the visitors began to filter through with their offerings stashed away in Sainsbury or St. Michael carriers, and, some few of them, with bunches of blooms for the newly hospitalised.

Life is, alas, so full of disappointments; and it was to be an unexpected visitor who was to monopolise

Morse's time that evening. Bearing a wilting collection of white chrysanthemums, a sombre-looking woman of late-middle age proceeded to commandeer the sole chair set at his bedside.

"Mrs. Green! How very nice of you to come!"

Morse's heart sank deeply, and took an even deeper plunge when the dutiful charlady mounted a sustained challenge against Morse's present competence to deal, single-handedly, with such crucial matters as towels, toothpaste, talcum-powder, and clean pyjamas (especially the latter). It was wonderfully good of her (who could deny it?) to take such trouble to come to see him (*three* buses, as Morse knew full well); but he found himself consciously *willing* her to get up and *go*.

At five minutes past eight, after half a dozen "I-really-must-go's, Mrs. G. rose to her poorly feet in preparation for her departure, with instructions for the care of the chrysanthemums. At last (at last!), after a mercifully brief account of her latest visit to her "sheeropodist" in Banbury Road, Mrs. G. dragged her long-suffering feet away from Ward 7C.

On several occasions, from her father's bedside, Christine Greenaway had half-turned in the course of her filial obligations; and two or three times her eyes had locked with Morse's; hers with the half-masked smile of understanding; his with all the impotence of some stranded whale.

Just as Mrs. Green was on her way, a white-coated consultant, accompanied by the Charge Nurse, decided (inconsiderately) to give ten minutes of his time to Greenaway Senior, and then in some *sotto voce* asides, to confide his prognosis to Greenaway Junior. And for Morse, this hiatus in the evening's ordering was getting just about as infuriating as waiting for breakfast in some "Fawlty Towers" hotel.

Then Lewis came.

Never had Morse been less glad to see his sergeant; yet he *had* instructed Lewis to pick up his post from the flat, and he now took possession of several envelopes and a couple of cards: Morse's shoes (his other pair) were now ready for collection from Grove Street; his car licence was due to be renewed within the next twenty days; a ridiculously expensive book on *The Transmission of Classical Manuscripts* now awaited him at OUP; a bill from the plumber for the repair of a malfunctioning stop-cock was still unpaid; the Wagner Society asked if he wanted to enter his name in a raffle for Bayreuth *Ring* tickets; and Peter Imbert invited him to talk in the new year at a weekend symposium, in Hendon, on inner-city crime. It was rather like a cross-section of life, his usual correspondence: half of it was fine, and half of it he wanted to forget.

At twenty-three minutes past eight, by the ward

clock, Lewis asked if there was anything else he could do.

"Yes, Lewis. Please *go*, will you? I want to have five minutes with—" Morse nodded vaguely over to Greenaway's bed.

"Well, if that's what you want, sir." He rose slowly to his feet.

"It *is* what I bloody want, Lewis! I've just *told* you, haven't I?"

Lewis took a large bunch of white seedless grapes (£2.50 a pound) from his carrier-bag. "I thought—we thought, the missus and me—we thought you'd enjoy them, sir."

He was gone; and Morse knew, within a second of his going, that he would not be forgiving himself easily for such monumental ingratitude. But the damage was done: *nescit vox missa reverti.*

The bell rang two minutes later, and Christine came across to Morse's bed as she left, and handed him six large photocopied sheets.

"I hope this is what you wanted."

"I'm ever so grateful. It's—it's a pity we didn't have a chance to . . ."

"I understand. I *do* understand," she said. "And you will let me know if I can do anything else?"

"Look . . . perhaps if we—"

"Come along now, please!" The Charge Nurse's voice sounded to Morse almost as imperious as Nessie's as she walked quickly around the beds.

"I'm so grateful," said Morse. "I really am! As I say, it's . . ."

"Yes," said Christine softly.

"Will you be in tomorrow?" asked Morse quickly.

"No—not tomorrow. We've got some librarians coming from California—"

"Come along now, *please*!"

Mrs. Green, Sergeant Lewis, Christine Greenaway—now all of them gone; and already the medicine-trolley had been wheeled into the ward, and the nurses were starting out on yet another circuit of measurements and medicaments.

And Morse felt sick at heart.

It was at 9:20 P.M. that he finally settled back against his piled pillows to glance quickly through the photo-copied material Christine had found for him. And soon he was deeply and happily engrossed—his temporary despondency departing on the instant.

Chapter Fourteen

> Being in the land of the living was itself the survivor's privilege, for so many of one's peers—one's brothers and sisters—had already fallen by the wayside, having died at birth, at infancy or childhood.
> (*Roy & Dorothy Porter*, In Sickness and In Health)

The documents which Morse now handled were just the thing (he had little doubt) for satisfying the original-source-material philosophy which was just then swamping the GCSE and A-level syllabuses. And for Morse, whose School Certificate in History (Credit) had demanded little more than semi-familiarity with the earliest models of seed-drills and similar agricultural adjuncts of the late eighteenth century, the reading of them was fascinating. Particularly poignant, as it appeared to Morse, was the Foreword to the *Insurance Guide and Hand-book 1860* (bless the girl!—she'd even got the exact year) where the anonymous author stated his own determination to soldier along in "this vale of tears" for as long as decently possible:

> Thus it is that all our efforts are forever required, not to surpass what we may call the biblical "par" for life—that famous "three-score years and ten"—but to come reasonably near to attaining it at all. For it is only by continuous vigilance and energy in the work for self preservation that the appointed average can be brought into view; and with good fortune and good sense (and God's grace) be achieved.

It was interesting to find the Almighty in parenthesis, even in 1860, and Morse felt he would like to have known the author. Yet when that same author went on to assert that "mortality had decreased by two-fifths between 1720 and 1820," Morse began to wonder what on earth such a bafflingly unscientific— indeed, quite nonsensical—statement might mean. What did seem immediately clear, as he read through the small print, was that people during those years were beginning to live rather longer, and that by the middle of the nineteenth century insurance companies were beginning to match this sociological phenomenon with increasingly attractive rates and premiums, in spite of the sombre statistics appended to each year, right up to the 1850s. Like 1853, e.g.—the figures for which Morse now considered. Of the half million or so departed souls reported in the pages of the Guide, 55,000 had died of consumption, 25,000 of pneumonia, 24,500 of convulsions, 23,000 of bronchitis, 20,000 of premature death and debility, 19,000 of typhus, 16,000 of scarlatina, 15,000 of diarrhoea, 14,000 of heart disease, 12,000 of whooping cough, 11,000 of dropsy, 9,000 of apoplexy, 8,500 of paralysis, 6,000 of asthma, 5,750 of cancer, 4,000 of teeth troubles, 3,750 of measles, 3,500 of croup, 3,250 of small pox, 3,000 of (mothers) giving birth; and so on to the smaller numbers succumbing to diseases of brain, kidney, liver, and other perishable parts of the anatomy—and to old age! As he added up such numbers quickly in his head, Morse realised that about two-thirds of the 500,000 were unaccounted for; and he had to assume that even with a few more categories added ("murder" for one!) there must have been vast numbers of people in those days whose deaths were for some reason or other not specifically "accounted for" at all, albeit being registered in the national statistics. Perhaps a lot of them were just not important enough to get their own particular malady spelled out on any death certificate; perhaps many of the physicians, mid-wives, nurses, poor-law-attendants, or whatever, just didn't know, or didn't want to know, or didn't care.

As he lay back in the pillows and thought of the circumstances besetting the luckless Joanna Franks, who had died neither of consumption nor pneumonia . . . nor . . . he suddenly fell into a sleep so deep that he missed his 10 P.M. Horlicks and his treasured digestive biscuit; and then he woke up again, somewhat less than refreshed, at ll.45 P.M., with a dry throat and a clear head. The lights in the ward were turned down to half power, and the other patients around him seemed contentedly asleep— apart from the man who'd been admitted late that afternoon and around whom the medical staff had been fussing with a rather ominous concern; the man who now lay staring at the ceiling, doubtless contemplating the imminent collapse of his earthly fortunes.

Nessie was nowhere to be seen: the desk was empty.

He'd just had a nasty little dream. He'd been playing cricket in his early days at Grammar School; and when it came to his turn to bat, he couldn't find his boots . . . and then when he did find them the laces kept snapping; and he was verging on a tearful despair—when he'd awoken. It might have been Mrs. Green talking about her chiropody? Or was it Lewis, perhaps, who'd brought the card from the cobblers? Or neither of them? Was it not more likely to have been a young woman in 1859 who'd shouted, with her particular brand of terrified despair, "What have you done with my shoes?"

He looked around again: the desk was still empty.

Surely he wasn't likely to imperil the well-being of the ward if he turned on his angle-lamp? Especially if focused directly into a small pool of light on his own pillows? No! Reading a book wasn't going to hurt anyone and the sick man had had *his* light on all the time.

Pushing in the button switch, he turned on his own light, with no reaction from anyone; and still no sign of Nessie.

Part Three of *Murder on the Oxford Canal* was close to hand; but Morse was reluctant to finish *that* too quickly. He remembered when he'd first read *Bleak House* (still to his mind the greatest novel in the English language) he'd deliberately decelerated his reading as the final pages grew ever thinner beneath his fingers. Never had he wanted to hang on to a story so much! Not that the Colonel's work was anything to wax all that lyrical about; and yet Morse *did* want to eke it out—or so he told himself. Which left the not displeasing possibility of a few further chapters of *The Blue Ticket*—with Mr. Greenaway now fast asleep. The pattern of crime in nineteenth-century Shropshire had already joined the local legion of lost causes.

Morse was soon well into the exploits of a blonde who would have had arrows on her black stockings pointing northward and reading "This way for the knickers"—that is, if she'd worn any stockings; or worn any knickers, for that matter. And it was amid much parading of bodies, pawing of bosoms, and patting of buttocks, that Morse now spent an enjoyable little interval of erotic pleasure; indeed, was so engrossed that he did not mark her approach.

"What do you think you're doing?"

"I was just—"

"Lights go out at ten o'clock. You're disturbing everyone on the ward."

"They're all asleep."

"Not for much longer, with you around!"

"I'm sorry—"

"What's this you're reading?"

Before he could do anything about it, Nessie had removed the book from his hands, and he had no option but to watch her helplessly. She made no comment, passed no moral judgement, and for a brief second Morse wondered if he had not seen a glint of some semi-amusement in those sharp eyes as they had skimmed a couple of paragraphs.

"Time you were asleep!" she said, in a not unkindly fashion, handing him back the book. Her voice was as crisp as her uniform, and Morse replaced the ill-starred volume in his locker. "And be careful of your fruit juice!" She moved the half-filled glass one millimetre to the left, turned off the light, and was gone. And Morse gently eased himself down into the warmth and comfort of his bed,

like Tennyson's lily sliding slowly into the bosom of
the lake . . .

That night he dreamed a dream in Technicolor (he
swore it!), although he knew such a claim would be
contradicted by the oneirologists. He saw the ochre-
skinned, scantily clad siren in her black, arrowed
stockings, and he could even recall her lavender-
hued underclothing. Almost it was the perfect
dream! Almost. For there was a curiously insistent
need in Morse's brain which paradoxically demanded a *factual* name and place and time before, in
fantasy, that sexually unabashed freebooter could
be his. And in Morse's muddled computer of a mind,
that siren took the name of one Joanna Franks,
provocatively walking along towards Duke's Cut, in
the month of June in 1859.

When he awoke (was woken, rather) the following
morning, he felt wonderfully refreshed, and he resolved that he would take no risks of any third
humiliation over *The Blue Ticket*. With breakfast,
temperature, wash, shave, blood-pressure, newspaper,
tablets, Bovril, all these now behind him—and with
not a visitor in sight—he settled down to discover exactly what had happened to that young woman who
had taken control of his nocturnal fantasies.

Chapter Fifteen

PART THREE
A Protracted Trial

Joanna Franks's body was found at Duke's Cut at
about 5:30 A.M. on Wednesday, 22nd June 1859.
Philip Tomes, a boatman, said he was passing
down-canal towards Oxford when he saw something in the water—something which was soon
identified as, in part, a woman's gown; what else,
though, he could not for the moment make out
in the darkened waters. The object was on the
side of the canal opposite the tow-path, and in
due course he discovered it to be the body of a
female, without either bonnet or shoes. She was
floating alongside the bank, head north, feet
south, and there was no observable movement
about her. She was lying on her face, which
seemed quite black. Tomes stopped his boat, and

with a boat-hook gently pulled the body to the tow-path side, where he lifted it out of the water, in which latter task he was assisted by John Ward, a Kidlington fisherman, who happened to be passing alongside the canal at that early hour. In fact, it was Ward who had the presence of mind to arrange for the body, which was still warm, to be taken down to the Plough Inn at Wolvercote.

It appears from various strands of inter-weaving evidence, albeit some of it from the guilty parties themselves, that Oldfield and Musson (and, by one account, Towns also) left the *Barbara Bray* at roughly the point where Joanna met her death, and that they were seen standing together on the tow-path side of the canal just below Duke's Cut. A certain man passed by the area at the crucial time, 4 A.M. or just after, and both Oldfield and Musson, with great presence of mind, asked him if he had seen a woman walking beside the canal. The man had replied, as they clearly recalled, with a very definite "No!" and had made to get further on his way with all speed. Yet the two (or perhaps three) men had asked him the same question again and again, in rather an agitated manner.

(It is clear that this man's testimony could have been vital in substantiating the boatmen's claims. But he was never traced, in spite of wide-

scale enquiries in the area. A man roughly answering his description, one Donald Favant, had
signed the register at the Nag's Head in Oxford
for either the 20th or the 21st June—there was
some doubt—but this man never came forward.
The strong implication must therefore remain,
as it did at the time, that the whole story was the
clever concoction of desperate men.)

Jonas Bamsey, wharfinger in the employ of
the Oxford Canal Authority at Oxford's Hayfield
Wharf, gave evidence at the trial that the *Barbara Bray* had duly effected its partial unload-
ing, but that Oldfield had not reported the loss
of any passenger—which quite certainly should
have been the duty of the boat's captain under
the Authority's Regulations. Instead, according
to the scant and inconsistent evidence at this
point, the boatmen do appear to have confided
in some of their acquaintances in Upper Fisher
Row, claiming that their passenger had been out
of her mind; that she had committed suicide; and
that on at least one occasion they had been
called upon to save her from an attempted
drowning on the journey down from Preston
Brook.

Later that dreadful day, when the crew of the
Barbara Bray came to negotiate the lock on
the Thames at Iffley, two miles downstream
from Folly Bridge, Oldfield spoke to the keeper,

Albert Lee, and reported to him and his wife (co-incidentally also named Joanna) that a passenger on his boat had been drowned; but that she was most sadly deranged, and had been a sore trial to him and his fellow crew-members ever since she had first embarked at Preston Brook. Oldfield was still obviously very drunk. Pressed to explain what he was seeking to say, Oldfield asserted only that "It was a very bad job that had happened." The passenger was "off her head" and had been last seen by the crew off Gibraltar Lock. Yet Oldfield was vehemently unwilling to listen to Lee's suggestion of returning to Oxford to sort out the whole tragedy; and this made Lee more than somewhat suspicious. On the departure of the *Barbara Bray*, therefore, he himself immediately set off for Oxford, where he contacted the Pickford Office; and where the Pickford Office, in turn, contacted the Police Authority.

When the infamous boat finally arrived at Reading (for some reason, over two hours behind schedule) Constable Harrison was on hand, with appropriate support, to take the entire crew into custody, and to testify that all of them, including the youth, were still observably drunk and excessively abusive as he put them in darbies and escorted them to temporary cell-accommodation in the gaol at Reading. One of them, as Harrison vividly recalled, was vile enough to repeat some of his earlier invective against Joanna Franks, and was heard to mutter "Damn and blast that wicked woman!"

Hannah MacNeill, a serving woman at the Plough Inn, Wolvercote, testified that when the sodden body had been brought from the canal, she had been employed, under direction, to take off Joanna's clothes. The left sleeve was torn out of its gathers and the cuff on the same hand was also torn. Tomes and Ward, for their part, were quite firm in their evidence that they themselves had made no rips or tears in Joanna's clothing as they lifted her carefully from the water at Duke's Cut.

Katharine Maddison testified that she was a co-helper with Hannah MacNeill in taking off Joanna's drenched garments. Particularly had she noticed the state of Joanna's calico knickers which had been ripped right across the front. This garment was produced in Court; and many were later to agree that the production of such an intimate item served further to heighten the universal feeling of revulsion against those callous men who were now arraigned with her murder.

Mr. Samuels, the Oxford surgeon who examined the body at the inquest, reported signs of bruising below the elbow of the left arm, and further indications of subcutaneous bruising below the left and right cheekbones; the same man described the dead woman's face as presenting a state of "discoloration and disfigurement." Mr. Samuels agreed that it was perhaps possible for the facial injuries, such as they were, to have been caused by unspecified and accidental incidents in the water, or in the process of taking-up from the water. Yet such a possibility was now seeming, both to Judge and Jury, more and more remote.

The youth Wootton then gave his version of the tragic events, and on one point he expressed himself forcefully: that Towns had got himself "good and half-seas-over" the night before Joanna was found, and that he was sound asleep at the time the murder must have occurred, for he (Wootton) had heard him "snoring loudly." We shall never be in a position to know whether Towns had forced Wootton to give this evidence to the Court—under some threat or other, perhaps. From subsequent developments, however, it seems clear that we may give a substantial degree of credence to Wootton's testimony.

Joseph Jarnell, the co-prisoner pending whose evidence the re-trial had been agreed, related to the Court the damning confessions Oldfield had betrayed whilst the two men shared a prison-cell. In essence such "confessions" amounted to a rather crude attempt on Oldfield's part to settle the majority of blame for almost everything which had happened on Musson and Towns. But in spite of the man's earnest manner and the consistency of his account, Jarnell's story made little or no impression. Yet his testimony carried interest, if not conviction. Amongst the strongest of the fabrications which Oldfield had sought to put about was that Joanna Franks had in excess of fifty golden sovereigns in one of her two boxes; that Towns had discovered this fact, and that Joanna had found him rummaging through her trunks. She had threatened (so the allegation ran) to report him to the next Pickford Office if he did not mend his ways and make immediate apology and restoration. (Such nonsense was wholly discredited at the time, and may be safely discounted now.)

Together with many other items, the knife which Joanna had been observed sharpening was later found in one of her trunks, the cord of which had been cut, and which still remained untied. The assumption was that at some point the men had opened Joanna's belongings after the murder, and had replaced the knife in one of the trunks. It must certainly be considered a strong possibility that the men intended to steal some of her possessions, for as we have seen a charge of theft was included, in the most strongly worded terms, in the original indictment of the crew at the first trial in August 1859. It seems, however, that Prosecuting Counsel at the second trial were sufficiently confident to forego such a charge and to concentrate their accusations on murder, since the lesser charge (difficult, in any case, as it would have been to substantiate) was subsequently excluded. We have seen a similar procedure operating, in the first trial, concerning the charges of rape; and perhaps it is of some strange and macabre interest to note that in the original trial the charges of both rape and theft (as well as murder) were made against each individual member of the crew—including the young Wootton.

Out of all the evidence given at that memorable second trial at Oxford in April 1860, fairly certainly that of Charles Franks himself evoked the greatest feeling and the widest sympathy. The poor man was weeping aloud as he entered the witness-box, and it seemed as if it were almost beyond his physical powers to raise his eyes in order to bear the sight of the prisoners and to look upon their faces. He had obviously been deeply in love with Joanna, and turning his back on the vile men arraigned before the Court he explained how in consequence of some information he had come into Oxfordshire and seen his wife's dead body at the time of the inquest.

For although it was dreadfully disfigured (here the poor fellow could not at all restrain his feelings) yet he knew it by a small mark behind his wife's left ear, a mark of which only a parent or an intimate lover could have known. Corroboration of identification (if, in fact, corroboration was needed) was afforded by the shoes, later found in the fore-cabin of the *Barbara Bray*, which matched in the minutest degrees the contours of the dead woman's feet.

At the conclusion of the hearing, and after a lengthy summing-up by Mr. Augustus Benham, the Jury, under their duly appointed chairman, begged permission of his Lordship to retire to consider their verdict.

Chapter Sixteen

Perhaps it was the dream.

Whatever it was, Morse knew that something had at last prodded him into a slightly more intelligent appraisal of the Colonel's story, because he was now beginning to take account of two or three major considerations which had been staring at him all the while.

The first of these was the character of Joanna Franks herself. How had it come about—whatever the fortuitous, involuntary, or deliberate circumstances in which Joanna had met her death—that the crew of the *Barbara Bray* had insisted time and time again that the wretched woman had been nothing but one long, sorry trial to them all ever since she'd first jumped on board at Preston Brook? How *was* it that they were still damning and blasting the poor woman's soul to eternity way, way *after* they had pushed her into the Canal and, for all Morse or anyone else knew, held her head under the black waters until she writhed in agony against their murderous hands no longer? Had a satisfactory explanation been forthcoming for such events? All right, there was still Part Four of the story to come. But so far, the answer was "no."

There was, though (as it now occurred to Morse), one possible dimension to the case that the good Colonel had never even hinted at—either through an excessive sense of propriety, or from a lack of imagination—namely that *Joanna Franks had been a seductive tease*: a woman who over those long hours of that long journey had begun to drive the crew towards varied degrees of insanity with her provocative overtures, and to foster the inevitable jealousies arising therefrom.

Come off it, Morse!

Yes, come off it! There was no evidence to support such a view. None! Yet the thought stayed with him, reluctant to leave. An attractive woman . . . boredom . . . drink . . . a tunnel . . . continued boredom . . . more drink . . . another tunnel . . . dark-

ness . . . desire . . . opportunity . . . still more drink . . .
and more Priapic promptings in the loins . . . Yes, all
that, perhaps, the Colonel himself may have understood. But what if she, Joanna herself, had been the
active catalyst in the matter? What if she had craved
for the men just as much as they had craved for her?
What (put it simply, Morse!) *what if she'd wanted sex
just as badly as they did?* What if she were the precur-
sor of Sue Bridehead in *Jude the Obscure*, driving
poor old Phillotson potty, as well as poor old Jude?

"Men's questions!" he heard a voice say. "Just
the sort of thoughts that would occur to an ageing
MCP like you!"

There was a second general consideration which,
from the point of view of criminal justice, struck
Morse as considerably more cogent and a good
deal less contentious. In the court-room itself, the
odds did seem, surely, to have been stacked pretty
heavily against the crew of the *Barbara Bray*—with
"presumption of innocence" playing decidedly second fiddle to "assumption of guilt." Even the fair-
minded Colonel had let his prejudgements run
away with him a little: already he'd decided that
any ostensible concern on the part of the boatmen
for the missing passenger (believed drowned?)
was only shown "with great presence of mind" in
order to establish a semi-convincing alibi for
themselves; already he'd decided that these same
boatmen, "still obviously very drunk" (and by

implication still knocking it back at top-tipplers' rates) had manoeuvred their "infamous" craft down the Thames to Reading without having the common decency to mention to anyone the little matter of the murder they'd committed on the way. Did (Morse asked himself) wicked men tend to get more *drunk*—or more *sober*—after committing such callous crimes? Interesting thought . . .

Yes, and there was a third general point—one that seemed to Morse most curious: the charges both of Theft and of Rape had, for some reason, been dropped against the boatmen. Was this because the Prosecution had been wholly confident, and decided to go for the graver charge of Murder—with the expectation (fully justified) that they had sufficient evidence to convict "Rory" Oldfield and Co. on the capital indictment? Or was it, perhaps, because they had too *little* confidence in their ability to secure conviction on the *lesser* charges? Obviously, as Morse seemed vaguely to remember from his schooldays, neither rape nor theft would have been considered too venial an offence in the middle of the last century, but . . . Or was it just possible that these charges were dropped because there was no convincing evidence to support them? And if so, was the indictment for murder entered upon by the Prosecution for one simple reason—that it presented the *only* hope of bringing those miserable men to justice? Certainly, as far as multiple rape was concerned, the evidence must have been decidedly dodgy—as the Judge in the first trial had pronounced. But what about theft? The prerequisite of theft was that the aggrieved party possessed something worth the stealing. So what was it that poor Joanna had about her person, or had in either of her two travelling-boxes, that was worth the crime? The evidence, after all, pointed to the fact that she hadn't got a couple of pennies to rub together. Her fare for the canal-trip had been sent up from her husband in London; and even facing the terrible risks of travelling with a drunken, lecherous crew—certainly after Banbury had been reached—she had *not* taken, or not been *able* to take, any alternative means of transport to get to the husband who was awaiting her in the Edgware Road. So? So what had she got, if anything, that was worth stealing?

There were those shoes again, too! Did Joanna deliberately leave off her shoes? Did she enjoy the feel of the mud between her toes along the tow-path—like some bare-foot hippie on a watery walk round Stonehenge in the dawn?

What a strange case it had been! The more he thought about it, the greater the number of questions that kept occurring to Morse's mind. He had a good deal of experience in cases where the forensic and pathological evidence had been vital to the outcome of a court case. But he wasn't particularly impressed with the conclusions that (presumably) must have been drawn from Mr. Samuels' comparatively scientific findings. For Morse (wholly, it must be admitted, without medical or scientific qualifications) the state of the dress, and the bruising described, would have been much more consistent with Joanna being held firmly from behind, with the assailant's (?) left hand gripping her left wrist; and his (her?) right hand being held forcibly across her mouth, where thumb and forefinger would almost invariably produce the sort of bruising mentioned in the recorded description.

What of this Jarnell fellow? The Prosecution must have been considerably impressed, at the first hearing, with his potential testimony. Why, otherwise, would anyone be willing to postpone a trial for six months—on the word of a gaolbird? Even the Colonel had given the fellow a good write-up! So why was it that when he duly turned up to tell his tale, at the second trial, no one wished to listen to him? Had there been something, some knowledge, somewhere, that had caused the court to discount, or at least discredit, the disclosures his cellmate, Oldfield, had allegedly made to him? Because whatever accusations could be levelled against Oldfield, the charge of inconsistency was *not* amongst them. On three occasions, after Joanna's death, he had insisted that she was "out of her mind," "sadly deranged," "off her head" . . . And there had, it appeared, been no conflict of evidence between the crewmen that on one occasion at least (did that mean two?) they had been called upon to save Joanna from drowning herself. The one vital point Jarnell disclosed was that Oldfield had not only protested his own innocence of the murder, but had also sought to shift all responsibility on to his fellow crewmen. Not, to be sure, a very praise-worthy piece of behaviour! Yet, *if Oldfield himself were innocent*, where else could he have laid the blame? At the time, in any case, no one had been willing to listen seriously either to what Jarnell or to what Oldfield might have to say. But if they were right? Or if *one* of them were right?

A curious little thought struck Morse at this point, and lodged itself in a corner of his brain—for future reference. And a rather bigger thought struck him simultaneously: that he needed to re-member he was only playing a game with himself; only trying to get through a few days' illness with a happy little problem to amuse himself with—like a tricky cryptic crossword from *The Listener*. It was just a little worrying, that was all . . . the way the dice had been loaded all the time against those drunkards who had murdered Joanna Franks.

And the niggling doubt persisted.

If they had . . .

Chapter Seventeen

> The detective novelist, as a class, hankers after complication and ingenuity, and is disposed to reject the obvious and acquit the accused if possible. He is uneasy until he has gone further and found some new and satisfying explanation of the problem.
>
> (*Dorothy L. Sayers*, The Murder of Julia Wallace)

The thought that the crewmen may not have been guilty of Joanna Franks's murder proved to be one of those heady notions that evaporate in the sunrise of reason. For if the crewmen had not been responsible, who on earth had? Nevertheless, it seemed to Morse pretty much odds-on that if the case had been heard a century later, there would have been no certain conviction. Doubtless, at the time, the jury's verdict had looked safe and satisfactory, especially to the hostile crowds lining the streets and baying for blood. But *should* the verdict have been reached? True, there was enough circumstantial suspicion to sentence a saint; yet no really *direct* evidence, was there? No witnesses to murder; no indication of *how* the murder had been committed; no adequately convincing motive for *why*. Just a time, and a place, and Joanna lying face-downwards in Duke's Cut all that while ago.

Unless, of course, there were some passages of evidence not reported—either from the first or the second trial? The Colonel had clearly been rather more interested in the lax morals of the boatmen than in any substantiation of the evidence, and he could just have omitted the testimony of any corroborative witnesses who might have been called. Perhaps it would be of some interest—in this harmless game he was playing—to have a quick look through those Court Registers, if they still existed; or through the relevant copies of *Jackson's Oxford Journal*, which certainly *did* exist, as Morse knew, filed on microfiche in the Oxford Central Library. (Doubtless in the Bodley, too!) And, in any case, he hadn't finished the Colonel's book yet. Why, there might be much still to be revealed in that last exciting episode!

Which he now began to read.

Almost immediately he was conscious of Fiona standing beside him—the amply bosomed Fiona, smelling vaguely of the summer and strongly of disinfectant. Then she sat down on the bed, and he felt the pneumatic pressure of her against him as she leaned across and looked over his shoulder.

"Intereeeesting?"

Morse nodded. "It's the book the old girl brought round—you know, the Colonel's wife."

Fiona stayed where she was, and Morse found himself reading the same short sentence for the third, fourth, fifth time—without the slightest degree of comprehension—as her softness gently pressed against him. Was she conscious, herself, of taking the initiative in such memorable intimacy, however mild?

Then she ruined everything.

"I don't go in much for reading these days. Last book I read was *Jane Eyre*—for GCSE, that was."

"Did you enjoy it?" (Poor, dear Charlotte had long had a special place in Morse's heart.)

"Pretty boring stuff. We just had to do it, you know, for the exam."

Oh dear!

Crossing her black-stockinged legs, she took off one of her flat-heeled black shoes, and shook out some invisible irritant on to the ward floor.

"When do people take their shoes off?" asked Morse. "Normally, I mean?"

"Funny question, isn't it?"

"When they've a stone in them—like you?"

Fiona nodded. "And when they go to bed."

"And?"

"Well—when they go paddling at Blackpool."

"Yes?"

"When they sit watching the telly with their feet on the sofa—if they've got a mum as fussy as mine."

"Anything else?"

"What do you want to know all this for?"

"If they've got corns or something," persisted Morse, "and go to the chiropodist." ("Kyropodist," in Morse's book.)

"Yes. Or if their feet get sore or tired. Or if they have to take their tights off for some reason—"

"Such as?"

Morse saw the flash of sensuous amusement in her eyes, as she suddenly stood up, pulled his sheets straight, and shook out his pillows. "Well, if you don't know at your age—"

Oh dear!

Age.

Morse felt as young as he'd ever done; but suddenly, and so clearly, he could see himself as he *was* seen by this young girl.

Old!

But his mood was soon to be brightened by the totally unexpected re-appearance of Sergeant Lewis, who explained that the purpose of his unofficial visit (it was 2:15 P.M.) was to interview a woman, still in intensive care, in connection with yet another horrendous crash on the A34.

"Feeling OK this morning, sir?"

"I shall feel a jolly sight better once I've had the chance of apologising to you—for being so bloody ungrateful!"

"Oh yes? When was that, sir? I thought you were always ungrateful to me."

"I'm just sorry, that's all," said Morse simply and quietly.

Lewis, whose anger had been simmering and spitting like soup inadvertently left on the stove, had come into the ward with considerable reluctance. Yet when some ten minutes later he walked out, he felt the same degree of delight he invariably experienced when he knew that Morse needed *him*— even if it were only, as in this case, to do a bit of mundane research (Morse had briefly explained the case) and to try to discover if the Court Registers of the Oxford Assizes, 1859–60, were still available; and if so to see if any records of the trials were still extant.

After Lewis had gone, Morse felt very much more in tune with the universe. Lewis had forgiven him, readily; and he felt a contentment which he, just as much as Lewis, could ill define and only partly comprehend. And with Lewis looking into the Court Registers, there was another researcher in the field: a qualified librarian, who could very quickly sort out *Jackson's Oxford Journals*. Not that she was coming in that evening, alas!

Patience, Morse!

At 3 P.M. he turned once again to the beginning of the fourth and final episode in the late Colonel Deniston's book.

Chapter Eighteen

PART FOUR
A Pronounced Sentence

A bailiff was sworn in to attend the Jury, who immediately retired to the Clerk of Indictments' Room. After an absence of three-quarters of an hour, they returned to the Court; and, their names having been read over, every person appeared to wait with breathless anxiety for their verdict. In reply to the usual questions from Mr. Benham, the foreman replied that the Jury was all agreed and that they were unanimous in finding each of the three prisoners at the bar GUILTY of the murder of Joanna Franks. It is said that no visible alteration marked the countenances of the crew on the verdict being given, except that Oldfield for the moment became somewhat paler.

The black coif, emblematical of death, was placed on the Judge's head; and after asking the prisoners if they had anything to say, he passed his sentence in the following awesome terms:

Jack Oldfield, Alfred Musson, Walter Towns—after a long and patient hearing of the circumstances in this case, and after due deliberation on the part of the Jury, you have each and all of you been found guilty of the most foul crime of murder—the murder of an unoffending and helpless woman who was under your protection and who, there is now no doubt as to believe, was the object of your lust; and thereafter, to prevent detection of your crime, was the object of your cruelty. Look not for pardon in this world! Apply to the God of Mercy for that pardon which He alone can extend to sinners who are penitent for their misdeeds, and henceforth prepare yourselves for the ignominious death which now awaits you. This case is one of the most painful, the most disgusting, and the most shocking, that has ever come to my knowledge, and it must remain only for me to pass upon you the terrible and just sentence of the Law, that you be taken whence you came, and from thence to the place of execution, and that you, and each of you, be hanged by the neck until you be dead, and that your bodies be afterward buried within the precincts of the

prison and be not accorded the privilege of con-
secrated ground. And may God have mercy on
your souls!

After the trial was over, and sentence pronounced, the three men still persisted in main-
taining their innocence. Indeed, Oldfield's wife,
who visited the prison, was so agitated by her
husband's protestations that "she herself was
thrown into a sore fit."

It had seemed reasonably clear from various
statements, including those of Oldfield and
Musson, that Towns had been somewhat less involved in the happenings on the canal journey
than the other two. It was no surprise, therefore,
that some members of the legal profession now
thought there was a case for the last-minute re-
consideration of the sentence imposed upon
Towns; so a letter setting forth their agreed view
was taken to London by a barrister, and a special
interview with the Secretary of State was obtained. As a result of such representations, Towns
was reprieved at (almost literally) the eleventh
hour. The good news was broken to him as the
three men were receiving for the last time the
Holy Sacrament from the Prison Chaplain. Towns
immediately burst into a flood of tears, and taking each of his former associates by the hand
kissed them affectionately, repeating "God bless

you, dear friend!" "God bless you, dear friend!" He
was later transported to Australia for life, where
he was still alive in 1884 when he was seen and in-
terviewed by one Samuel Carter (like Oldfield
and Towns, a citizen of Coventry), who took a
lively interest in local history and who wrote
of his experiences on his return to England the
following year.[1]

Oldfield and Musson were duly hanged in public at Oxford. According to the newspaper reports, as many as ten thousand people were
estimated to have witnessed the macabre spectacle. It is reported that from an early hour men
sat high on walls, climbed trees, and even perched
on the roofs of overlooking houses in order to
obtain a good view of those terrible events. A
notice-board placed by the Governor in front of
the gaol door stated that the execution would
not proceed until after eleven o'clock; but although this occasioned much disappointment
among the spectators, it did not deter their continued attendance, and not a spare square-foot
of space was to be found when, at the appointed
hour, the execution finally occurred.

First to appear was the Prison Chaplain,
solemnly reading the funeral service of the

[1] *Travels and Talks in the Antipodes*, Samuel Carter (Farthinghill
Press, Nottingham, 1886).

Church of England; next came the two culprits; and following them the Executioner, and the Governor, as well as some other senior officers from the prison. After the operation of pinioning had been completed, the two men walked with firm step to the platform, and ascended the stairs to the drop without requiring assistance. When the ropes had been adjusted round their necks, the Executioner shook hands with each man; and then, as the Chaplain intoned his melancholy service, the fatal bolt was drawn, and in a minute or two, after much convulsion, the wretched malefactors were no more. The dislocation of the cervical vertebrae and the rupture of the jugular vein had been, if not an instantaneous, at least an effective procedure. The gallows appeared to have sated the sadistic fascination of the mob once more, for there are no reports of any civic disorders as the great throng dispersed homewards on that sunlit day. It was later disclosed, though it had not been observable at the time, that Oldfield's last action in life had been to hand over to the Chaplain a postcard, to be delivered to his young wife, in which to the very end he proclaimed his innocence of the crime for which he had now paid the ultimate penalty.

Locally produced broadsheets, giving every sensational detail of trial and execution, were

very quickly on sale in the streets of Oxford—
and were selling fast. They were even able to
give a full account, with precise biblical reference,
of the last sermon preached to the men at 6 P.M.
on the Sunday before their hangings. The text,
clearly chosen with ghoulish insensitivity, could
hardly have brought the condemned prisoners
much spiritual or physical solace: "Yet they
hearkened not unto me, nor inclined their ear,
but hardened their neck: they did worse than
their fathers" (*Jeremiah*, ch.7, v. 26).

The horror felt by the local population at the
murder of Joanna Franks did not end with the
punishment of the guilty men. Many, both lay
and clerical, thought that something more must
be done to seek to improve the morals of the
boatmen on the waterways. They were aware, of
course, that the majority of boatmen were called
upon to work on the Sabbath, and had therefore
little or no opportunity of attending Divine wor-
ship. A letter from the Revd. Robert Chantry,
Vicar of Summertown Parish, was typical of
many in urging a greater degree of concern
amongst the boatmen's employers, and suggesting some period of time free from duties on the
Sabbath to allow those having the inclination
the opportunity of attending a Church service.
Strangely enough, such attendance would have
been readily possible for the crew-members of

the *Barbara Bray* had Oxford been a regular
port-of-call, since a special "Boatmen's Chapel"
had been provided by Henry Ward, a wealthy
coal-merchant, in 1838—a floating chapel,
moored off Hythe Bridge, at which services were
held on Sunday afternoons and Wednesday
evenings. For Joanna Franks, as well as for her
sorrowing husband and parents, it was a human
tragedy that the sermon preached to the murderers on the Sunday prior to their execution
was perhaps the first—as well as the last—they
ever heard.

But it is all a long time ago now. The floating
chapel has long since gone; and no one today can
point with any certainty to the shabby plot in the
environs of Oxford Gaol where notorious criminals and murderers and others of the conjecturally damned were once buried.

Chapter Nineteen

> We read fine things but never feel them to the full until we have gone the same steps as the author.
> (*John Keats*, Letter to John Reynolds)

Morse was glad that the Colonel had ignored Doctor Johnson's advice to all authors that once they had written something particularly fine they should strike it out. For Part Four was the best-written section, surely, of what was proving to be one of the greatest assets in Morse's most satisfactory (so far) convalescence; and he turned back the pages to relish again a few of those fine phrases. Splendid, certainly, were such things as "sated the sadistic fascination"; and, better still, that "ghoulish insensitivity." But they were *more* than that. They seemed to suggest that the Colonel's sympathies had shifted slightly, did they not? Where earlier the bias against the boatmen had been so pronounced,

145

it appeared that the longer he went on the greater his compassion was growing for that disconsolate crew.

Like Morse's.

It was such a good *story*! So it was no surprise that the Colonel should have disinterred the bare bones of this particular one from the hundreds of other nineteenth-century burial-grounds. All the ingredients were there for its appealing to a wide readership, if once it got its foot wedged in the doorway of publicity. Beauty and the Beasts—that's what it was, quintessentially.

At least as the Colonel had seen it.

For Morse, who had long ago rejected the bland placebos of conventional religion, the facility offered to errant souls to take the Holy Sacrament before being strangled barbarously in a string seemed oddly at variance with the ban on the burial of these same souls within some so-called "holy ground." And he was reminded of a passage which had once been part of his mental baggage, the words of which now slowly returned to him. From *Tess of the d'Urbervilles*—where Tess herself seeks to bury her illegitimate infant in the place where "the nettles grow; and where all unbaptised infants, notorious drunkards, suicides, and others . . ." What was the end of it? Wasn't it—yes!—"others of the conjecturally damned are laid." Well, well! A bit of plagiarism on the Colonel's part. He really should have put quotation marks around that memorable phrase. Cheating just a little, really. Were there any other places where he'd cheated? Unwittingly, perhaps? Just a little?

Worth checking?

That floating chapel interested Morse, too, particularly since he had read something about it in a recent issue of *The Oxford Times*. He remembered, vaguely, that although the Oxford Canal Company gave regular monies towards its upkeep the boat on which it was housed had finally sunk (like the boatmen's hopes) and was terrestrialised, as it were, later in the century as a permanent chapel in Hythe Bridge Street; was now, at its latest conversion, metamorphosed to a double-glazing establishment.

Without looking back, Morse could not for the moment remember which of the other crew-members had been married. But it was good to learn that Oldfield's wife had stood beside her husband, for better or for worse. And a pretty bloody "worse" it had turned out to be! How interesting it would have been to know something of *her* story, too. How Morse would like to have been able to interview her, then and there! The recipient (presumably she had been) of that terrible card addressed to her, and handed to the Chaplain at the very foot of the gallows, she must have found it well-nigh impossible to believe that her husband could commit so foul a deed. But hers had been only a small rôle in the drama: only a couple of walking-on appearances, the first ending with a dead faint, and the second with a poignant little message from the grave. Morse nodded rather sadly to himself. These days there would be a legion of reporters from the *News of the World*, the *Sunday Mirror*, and the rest, hounding the life of the poor woman and seeking to prise out of her such vital information as whether he'd snored, or been tattooed on either upper or nether limbs, or how frequently they'd indulged in sexual intercourse, or what had been the usual greeting of the loving husband after coming back from one of his earlier murderous missions.

We live in a most degenerate age, decided Morse. Yet he knew, deep down, what nonsense such thinking was. He was no better himself, really, than one of those scandal-sheet scouts. He'd just confessed—had he not?—how much he himself wanted to interview Mrs. Oldfield and talk about all the things she must have known. And what (sobering thought!), what if *she* had invited each of them in, one after the other, separately—and asked for £20,000 a time?

No chance of any interview or talk now though—not with any of them ... But, suddenly, it struck Morse that perhaps there was: Samuel Carter's *Travels and Talks in the Antipodes*. That might be a most interesting document, surely? And (it struck Morse with particular pleasure) it would certainly be somewhere on the shelves of the three or four great UK libraries, the foremost of which was always going to be the Bodleian.

Lewis had already been given his research project; and work was now beginning to pile up for his second researcher in the field: what with *Jackson's Oxford Journal*, and now Carter's book . . . Had the Colonel consulted that? Must have done, Morse supposed—which was a little disappointing.

That Friday evening, Morse was visited by both Sergeant Lewis and Christine Greenaway, the latter suddenly changing her mind and foregoing a cocktail reception in Wellington Square. No trouble at all. Just the opposite.

Morse was very happy.

Chapter Twenty

As usual when she went into Oxford on a Saturday,
Christine Greenaway drove down to the Pear Tree
roundabout and caught the Park-and-Ride bus.
Alighting in Cornmarket, she walked up to Carfax, turned right into Queen's Street, and along
through the busy pedestrian precinct to Bonn
Square, where just past the Selfridges building she
pushed through the doors of the Westgate Central
Library. Among the wrong assumptions made by
Chief Inspector Morse the previous evening was
the fact that it would be sheer child's play for her to
fish out the fiche (as it were) of any newspaper ever
published, and that having effected such effortless
entry into times past she had the technical skill
and the requisite equipment to carry out some

immediate research. She hadn't told him that the Bodleian had not, to the best of her knowledge, ever micro-filmed the whole of the nation's press from the nineteenth century, nor that she herself was one of those people against whom all pieces of electrical gadgetry waged a non-stop war. She'd just agreed with him: yes, it would be a fairly easy job; and she'd be glad to help—again. To be truthful, though, she was. Earlier that morning she'd telephoned one of her acquaintances in the Reference Section of the Westgate Central, and learned that she could have immediate access to *Jackson's Oxford Journal* for 1859 and 1860. How long did she want to book things for? One hour? Two? Christine thought one hour would be enough.

10:30–11:30 A.M., then?

Perhaps Morse had been right all along. It *was* going to be easy.

On the second floor of the Central Library, in the Local History and Study Area, she was soon seated on an olive-green vinyl chair in front of a Micro-Film-Reader, an apparatus somewhat resembling the upper half of a British Telecom telephone-kiosk, with a vertical surface, some two feet square, facing her, upon which the photographed sheets of the newspaper appeared, in columns about 2½ inches wide. No lugging around or leafing through heavy bound-volumes of unmanageable newspapers. "Child's play." The controls marked Focusing Image, Magnification, and Light Control had all been pre-set for her by a helpful young library assistant (male), and Christine had only to turn an uncomplicated winding-handle with her right hand to skip along through the pages, at whatever speed she wished, of *Jackson's Oxford Journal*.

She was relieved, nevertheless, to discover that the Journal was a weekly, not a daily publication; and very soon she found the appropriate columns relating to the first trial of August 1859, and was making a series of notes about what she found; and, like Morse, becoming more and more interested. Indeed, by the time she had finished her research into the second trial, of April 1860, she was fascinated. She would have liked to go back and check up a few things, but her eyes were getting tired; and as soon as the print began to jump along like a line of soldiers dressing by the right, she knew that what the splendid machine called the Viewer Operator had better have a rest. She'd found a couple of pieces of information that might please Morse. She hoped so.

She was looking quickly through her scribbled notes, making sure that she could transcribe them later into some more legible form, when she became aware of a conversation taking place only three or four yards behind her at the Enquiries desk.

"Yes, I've tried County Hall—no help, I'm afraid."

"Your best bet I should think, then, is the City Archivists. They've got an office in—"

"They sent me here!"

"Oh!" The phone rang and the assistant excused himself to answer it.

Christine gathered up her notes, turned off the MFR (as it seemed to be known), and went up to the desk.

"We met yesterday evening—" began Christine.

Sergeant Lewis smiled at her and said, "Hullo."

"Seems I'm having more luck than you, Sergeant."

"Augh! He always gives me the lousy jobs—I don't know why I bother—my day off, too."

"And mine."

"Sorry we can't help, sir," said the assistant (another query dealt with). "But if they've got no trace at the Archivists . . ."

Lewis nodded. "Well, thanks, anyway."

Lewis escorted Christine to the swing doors when the assistant had a final thought: "You could try St. Aldates' Police Station. I *have* heard that quite a lot of documents and stuff got housed by the police in the war" ("Which war?" mumbled Lewis, inaudibly) "and, well, perhaps—"

"Thanks very much!"

"They can't really be *all* that helpful to the public, though—I'm sure you know—"

"Oh yes!"

But the phone had been ringing again, and now the assistant answered it, convinced that he'd sent his latest customer on what would prove a wholly unproductive mission.

When alone in crowded streets, Christine sometimes felt a little apprehensive; but she experienced a pleasing sense of being under protection as she walked back towards Carfax with the burly figure of Sergeant Lewis beside and above her. Great Tom was striking twelve noon.

"I don't suppose you fancy a drink—" began Lewis.

"No—not for me, thank you. I don't drink much, anyway, and it's a bit—bit early, isn't it?"

Lewis grinned: "That's something I don't hear very often from the Chief!" But he felt relieved. He wasn't much good at making polite conversation; and although she seemed a very nice young lady he preferred to get about his business now.

"You like him, don't you? The 'Chief,' I mean?"

"He's the best in the business."

"Is he?" asked Christine, quietly.

"Will you be going in tonight?"

"I suppose so. What about you?"

"If I find anything—which seems at the moment very doubtful."

"You never know."

Chapter Twenty-one

> From the cradle to the coffin, underwear comes first.
> (*Bertolt Brecht*, The Threepenny Opera)

In the late 1980s the premises of the City Police HQ in St. Aldates' were being extensively renovated and extended—and the work was still in progress when Sergeant Lewis walked in through the main door that Saturday morning. The Force had always retained its obstinately hierarchical structure, and friendships between the higher and the lower ranks would perhaps always be slightly distanced. Yet Lewis knew Chief Superintendent Bell fairly well from the old days up at Kidlington and was glad to find him in the station.

Yes, of course Bell would help if he could: in fact, the timing of Lewis's visit might be very opportune, because many corners and crannies had only just been cleared out, and the contents of scores of cupboards and dust-covered cases and crates had recently seen the light of day for the first time within living memory. Bell's orders on this had been clear: if any documents seemed even marginally worth the keeping, let them be kept; if not, let them be destroyed. But strangely, up to now, almost everything so newly rediscovered had appeared potentially valuable to *someone*; and the upshot was that a whole room had been set aside in which the preserved relics and mementos from the earliest days—certainly from the 1850s onwards—had been unsystematically stacked, awaiting appropriate evaluation by academic historians, sociologists, criminologists, local-history societies—and authors. In fact a WPC was in the room now, as Bell thought—doing a bit of elementary cataloguing; and if Lewis wanted to look around . . .

Explaining that this was her lunch-break, WPC Wright, a pleasant enough brunette in her mid-twenties, continued eating her sandwiches and writing her Christmas cards, waving Lewis to any quarter of the room he wished after he had briefly stated his mission.

"It's all yours, Sergeant. Or, at least, I wish it was!"

Lewis could see what she meant. Morse had given him a copy of the Colonel's work (several spares had been left on the ward); but for the moment Lewis could see little or no chance of linking anything that had occurred in 1860 with the chaotic heaps of boxes, files, bags, crates, and piles of discolored, dog-eared documents that lay around. To be fair, it was clear that a start had been made on sorting things out, for fifty-odd buff-coloured labels, with dates written on them, were attached to the rather neater agglomeration of material that had been separated from the rest, and set out in some semblance of chronological order. But amongst these labels Lewis looked in vain for 1859 or 1860. Was it worth having a quick look through the rest?

It was at 1:45 P.M., after what had proved to be a long look, that Lewis whistled softly.

"You found something?"

"Do you know anything about this?" asked Lewis. He had lifted from one of the tea-chests a chipped and splintered box, about two feet long, by one foot wide, and about 9–10 inches deep; a small box, by any reckoning, and one which could be carried by a person with little difficulty, since a brass plate, some 4 inches by half an inch, set in the middle of the box's top, held a beautifully moulded semi-circular handle, also of brass. But what had struck Lewis instantly—and with wondrous excitement—were the initials engraved upon the narrow plate: "J.D."! Lewis had not read the slim volume with any great care (or any great

interest, for that matter); but he remembered
clearly the two "trunks" which Joanna had taken
on to the boat and which presumably had been
found in the cabin after the crew's arrest. Up to that
point, Lewis had just had a vague mental picture of
the sort of "trunks" seen outside Oxford colleges
when the undergraduates were arriving. But surely
it had said that Joanna was *carrying* them, hadn't
it? And by the well-worn look of the handle it
looked as if this box had been carried—and carried
often. And the name of Joanna's first husband had
begun with a "D"!

The policewoman came over and knelt beside
the box. The two smallish hooks, one on each side
of the lid, moved easily; and the lock on the front
was open, for the lid lifted back to reveal, inside the
green-plush lining, a small canvas bag, on which,
picked out in faded yellow wool, were the same initials as on the box.

Lewis whistled once more. Louder.

"Can you—can we—?" He could scarcely keep
the excitement from his voice, and the policewoman looked at him curiously for a few seconds,
before gently shaking out the bag's contents on to
the floor: a small, rusted key, a pocket comb, a metal
spoon, five dress-buttons, a crochet-hook, a packet
of needles, two flat-heeled, flimsy-looking shoes,
and a pair of calico knickers.

Lewis shook his head in dumbfounded disbelief.

He picked up the shoes in somewhat gingerly fashion as if he suspected they might disintegrate; then, between thumb and forefinger, the calico knickers.

"Think I could borrow these shoes and the er . . . ?" he asked.

WPC Wright eyed him once again with amused curiosity.

"It's all right," added Lewis. "They're not for me."

"No?"

"Morse—I work for Morse."

"I suppose you're going to tell me he's become a knicker-fetishist in his old age."

"You know him?"

"Wish I did!"

"He's in hospital, I'm afraid—"

"Everybody says he drinks far too much."

"A bit, perhaps."

"Do you know him well, would you say?"

"Nobody knows him all *that* well."

"You'll have to sign for them—"

"Fetch me the book!"

"—and bring them back."

Lewis grinned. "They'd be a bit small for me, anyway, wouldn't they? The shoes, I mean."

Chapter Twenty-two

> Don't take action because of a name! A name is an uncertain thing, you can't count on it!
>
> (*Bertolt Brecht*, A Man's a Man)

During that same Saturday which saw Sergeant Lewis and Christine Greenaway giving up their free time on his behalf, Morse himself was beginning to feel fine again. Exploring new territory, too, since after lunchtime he was told he was now free to wander along the corridors at will. Thus it was that at 2:30 P.M. he found his way to the Day Room, an area equipped with armchairs, a colour TV, table-skittles, a book-case, and a great pile of magazines (the top one, Morse noted, a copy of *Country Life* dating from nine years the previous August). The room was deserted; and after making doubly sure the coast was clear, Morse placed one of the three books he was carrying in the bottom of the large wastepaper receptacle there: *The Blue Ticket* had brought him little but embarrassment and humiliation, and now, straightaway, he felt like Pilgrim after depositing his sackful of sin.

The surfaces of the TV set seemed universally smooth, with not the faintest sign of any switch, indentation, or control with which to set the thing going; so Morse settled down in an armchair and quietly contemplated the Oxford Canal once more.

The question for the Jury, of course, had not been "Who committed the crime?" but only "Did the prisoners do it?"; whilst for a policeman like himself the question would always have to be the first one. So as he sat there he dared to say to himself, honestly, "All right! If the boatmen didn't do it, *who did?*" Yet if that were now the Judge's key question, Morse couldn't see the case lasting a minute longer; for the simple answer was he hadn't the faintest idea. What he *could* set his mind to, though, was some considered reflection upon the boatmen's guilt. Or innocence . . .

A quartet of questions, then.

First. Was it true that a jury should have been satisfied, beyond any reasonable doubt, that the boatmen murdered Joanna Franks? Answer: no. Not one shred of positive evidence had been produced by the prosecution which could be attested in court by any corroborative witnesses to murder—and it had been on the count of murder that the boat-men had been convicted.

Second. Was it true that the prisoners at the bar had been afforded the time-honoured "presumption of innocence"—the nominal glory of the British Legal System? Answer: it most definitely was not. Prejudge-ments—wholly pejorative prejudgements—had been rife from the start of the first trial, and the attitude of the law officers no less than the general public had been, throughout, one of unconcealed contempt for, and revulsion against, the crude, barely literate, irreli-gious crew of the *Barbara Bray*.

Third. Was it true that the boatmen, or some of them, were likely to have been guilty of something? Answer: almost certainly, yes; and (perversely) most probably guilty on the two charges that were dropped—those of rape and theft. At the very least, there was no shortage of evidence to suggest that the men had lusted mightily after their passenger, and it was doubtless a real possibility that all three—all four?—had sought to force their advances on the hapless (albeit sexually provocative?) Joanna.

Fourth. Was there a general sense—even if the evidence *was* unsatisfactory, even if the Jury *were* unduly prejudiced—in which the verdict was a rea-sonable one, a "safe" one, as some of the juris-prudence manuals liked to call it? Answer: no, a thousand times no!

Almost, now, Morse felt he could put his finger on the major cause of his unease. It was all those conversations, heard and duly reported, between the principal characters in the story: conversations between the crew and Joanna; between the crew and other boatmen; between the crew and lock-keepers, wharfingers, and constables—all of it was *wrong* somehow. *Wrong, if they were guilty.* It was as if some inexperienced playwright had been given a murder-plot, and had then proceeded to write page after page of inappropriate, misleading, and occasionally contradictory dialogue. For there were moments when it looked as if it were Joanna Franks who was the avenging Fury, with the crew-men merely the victims of her fatal power.

Then, too, the behaviour of Oldfield and Musson *after* the murder seemed to Morse increasingly a matter of considerable surprise, and it was difficult to understand why Counsel for the Defence had not sought to ram into the minds of Judge and Jury alike the utter *implausibility* of what, allegedly, they did and said. It was not unknown, admittedly, for the odd psychopath to act in a totally irrational and irresponsible manner. But these men were *not* a quartet of psychopaths. And, above all, it seemed quite extraordinary to Morse that, even after (as was claimed) the crew had somehow and for some reason managed to murder Joanna Franks, they were—some twenty-four, thirty-six hours later—

still knocking back the booze, still damning and blasting the woman's soul to eternity. Morse had known many murderers, but never one who had subsequently acted in such a fashion—let alone *four*. No! It just didn't add up; didn't add up at all. Not that it mattered, though—not really—after all these years.

Morse flicked open the index of the stout volume recording the misdeeds of Old Salopians, and his eye caught "Shropshire Union Canal (The)." He turned idly to the page reference, and there read through the paragraph, and with growing interest. (Well done, Mrs. Lewis!) The author was still most horribly enmeshed in his barbed-wire style, still quite incapable of calling a spade anything else but a broad-bladed digging-tool; but the message was clear enough:

> With such an incidence of crime on the canals, it can scarcely be a source of surprise that we find countless instances of evasiveness, on the part of many of the boatmen, in matters such as the registering of names, both those of the boats they crewed and of their own persons. Specifically, with regard to the latter of these deceptions, we discover that many of those working both on the water and on the wharfs had a duality of names, and were frequently considerably better known by their "bye-names" than by their christened

nomenclature. For varied sociological reasons (some of which we have yet to analyse) it can more than tentatively be suggested that boatmen as a generality were likely to be potentially predisposed to the regular commission of crime, and certain it must be held that their profession (if such it may be called) afforded ample opportunities for the realisation of such potentiality. Sometimes they sold parts of their cargoes, replacing, for example, quantities of coal with similar quantities of rocks or stone; frequently we come across recorded instances (see esp. SCL, *Canal and Navigable Waters Commission*, 1842, Vol. IX, pp. 61–4, 72–5, 83–6, *et passim*) of crewmen drinking from their cargoes of fine wines and whiskies, and refilling the emptied bottles with water. Toll officials, too, do not always appear blameless in these affairs, and could occasionally be bribed into closing their eyes...

Morse's eyes were beginning to close, too, and he laid the book aside. The point had been made: boatmen were a load of crooks who often nicked bits of their cargoes. Hence Walter Towns, aka Walter Thorold, and the rest. All as simple as that—once you knew the answers. Perhaps it would *all* be like that one day, in that Great Computer Library in the Sky, when the problems that had beset countless generations of sages and philosophers would be answered immediately, just by tapping in the questions on some celestial key-board.

The youth with the portable saline-drip walked in, nodded to Morse, picked up a small TV control-panel from somewhere, and began flicking his way around the channels with, for Morse, irritating impermanence. It was time to get back to the ward.

As he was leaving his eyes roamed automatically over the book-case, and he stopped. There, on the lower row, and standing side by side, were the titles *Victorian Banbury* and *OXFORD (Rail Centres Series)*. Having extracted both, he walked back. Perhaps, if you kept your eyes open, you didn't need any Valhallan VDUs at all.

Walter Algernon Greenaway had been trying, with little success, to get going with *The Oxford Times* crossword. He had little or no competence in the skill, but it had always fascinated him; and when the previous day he had watched Morse complete *The Times* crossword in about ten minutes, he felt most envious. Morse had just settled back in his bed when Greenaway (predictably known to his friends, it appeared, as "Waggie") called across.

"You're pretty good at crosswords—"

"Not bad."

"You know anything about cricket?"

"Not much. What's the clue?"

" 'Bradman's famous duck.' "

"How many letters?"

"Six. I saw Bradman at the Oval in 1948. He got a duck then."

"I shouldn't worry too much about cricket," said Morse. "Just think about Walt Disney."

Greenaway licked the point of his pencil, and thought, unproductively, about Walt Disney.

"Who's the setter this week?" asked Morse.

"Chap called 'Quixote.' "

Morse smiled. Coincidence, wasn't it! "What was *his* Christian name?"

"Ah! I have you, sir!" said Waggie, happily entering the letters at 1 across.

Chapter Twenty-three

> All that mankind has done, thought, gained, or been, it is all lying in magic preservation in the pages of books.
>
> *(Thomas Carlyle)*

Embarras de richesses—for Morse couldn't have chosen a more informative couple of books if he'd sauntered all day round the shelves in the local Summertown Library.

First, from *Victorian Banbury*, he gleaned the information that by about 1850 the long-distance stage-coach routes via Banbury to London had been abandoned, almost entirely as a result of the new railway service from Oxford to the capital. Yet, as a direct result of this service, coaches between Banbury and Oxford had actually *increased*, and regular and efficient transportation was readily available between Banbury and Oxford (only

twenty miles to the south) during the 1850s and
1860s. Furthermore, the author gave full details of
the actual stage-coaches that would have been
available, on the day in question, and about which
Joanna Franks must have made enquiry: quite certainly coach-horses would have been seen galloping southwards on three separate occasions in the
earlier half of the following day, delivering passengers picked up at the Swan Inn, Banbury, to the Angel Inn in the High at Oxford. That for the sum of
2*s*/1*d*. Even more interesting for Morse was the
situation pertaining at Oxford itself, where trains to
Paddington, according to his second work of reference, were far more frequent, and far quicker, than
he could have imagined. And presumably Joanna
herself, at Banbury on that fateful day, had been
presented with *exactly* the same information: no
less than *ten* trains daily, leaving at 2:10 A.M.,
7:50 A.M., 9 A.M., 10:45 A.M., 11:45 A.M., 12:55 P.M.,
2:45 P.M., 4:00 P.M., 5:50 P.M., and 8:00 P.M. *Embarras
du choix.* Admittedly, the fares seemed somewhat
steep, with 1st-, 2nd-, and 3rd-class carriages priced
respectively at 16*s*, 10*s*, 6*s*, for the 60-odd-mile journey. But the historian of Oxford's railways was fair-
minded enough to add the fact that there were also
three coaches a day, at least up until the 1870s, making the comparatively slow journey to London via
the Henley and Reading turnpikes: *The Blenheim*
and *The Prince of Wales*, each departing at 10:30

A.M., with *The Rival* an hour later, the fare being a "whole shilling" less than the 3rd-class railway fare. And where did they finish up in the metropolis? It was quite extraordinary. The Edgware Road!

So, for a few minutes Morse looked at things from Joanna's point of view—a Joanna who (as he had no option but to believe) was *in extremis*. Arriving at Banbury, as she had, in the latish evening, she would very soon have seen the picture. No chance of anything immediately, but the ready opportunity of a stay overnight in Banbury, in one of the taverns along the quayside, perhaps. Not four-star AA accomodation—but adequate, and certainly costing no more than 2*s* or so. Then one of the coaches to Oxford next morning—the book of words mentioned one at 9:30 A.M., reaching Oxford at about 1 P.M. That would mean no difficulty at all about catching the 2:45 P.M. to Paddington—or one of the three later trains, should any accident befall the horses. Easy! If she *had* eventually made a firm decision to escape her tormentors for good, then the situation was straightforward. 2*s* overnight, say, 2*s*/1*d* coach-fare, 6*s* 3rd-class rail-fare—that meant that for about 10*s* she was offered a final chance of saving her life. And without much bother, without much expense, she *could* have done so.

But she hadn't. Why not? Received wisdom maintained that she hadn't got a penny-piece to her name, let alone half a guinea. But had she nothing she could sell, or pawn? Had she no negotiable property with her? What *had* she got in those two boxes of hers? Nothing of any value whatsoever? Why, then, if that were so, could there ever have been the slightest suspicion of *theft*? Morse shook his head slowly. Ye gods!—how he wished he could have a quick look into one of those boxes!

It was tea-time, and Morse was not aware that his wish had already been granted.

Chapter Twenty-four

Magnus Alexander corpore parvus erat (Even Alexander the Great didn't measure up to the height-requirement of the Police Force).

(Latin Proverb)

Normal shifts for the nursing staff at the JR2 were Early (07:45–15:45), Late (13:00–21:30), and Night (21:00–08:15). Always more of an owl than a lark, Eileen Stanton shared none of the common objections that were levelled against the Night shift: born with a temperament slightly tinged with melancholy, she was perhaps a natural creature of the dark. But this particular week had been unusual. And that day she was on Late.

Married at the age of nineteen and divorced at twenty, she was now, five years later, living out at Wantage with a man, fifteen years her senior, who had celebrated his fortieth birthday the previous evening (hence the re-arrangements). The party had gone splendidly until just after midnight when the celebrant himself had been involved in a pathetic little bout of fisticuffs, over *her*! Now, in films or on TV, after being knocked unconscious with a vicious blow from an iron bar, the hero has only to rub the sore spot for a couple of minutes before resuming his mission. But life itself, as Eileen knew, wasn't like that—the victim was much more likely to end up in the ICU, with permanent brain-damage, to boot. Much more cruel. Like last night (this morning!) when her cohabitee had been clouted in the face, his upper lip splitting dramatically, and one of his front teeth being broken off at the root. Not good for his looks, or his pride, or the party, or Eileen, or anybody. Not good at all!

For the umpteenth time her mind dwelt on that incident as she drove into Oxford, parked her apple-jack-green Metro in the Staff Only park of the JR2, and walked down to the Basement Cloak Room to change her clothes. It would do her good to get back on the Ward, she knew that. She'd found it easy enough so far to steer clear of any emotional involvement with her patients, and for the moment all she wanted was to get a few hours of dutiful nursing behind her—to forget the previous night, when she'd drunk a little too freely, and flirted far too flagrantly with a man she'd never even met before . . . No hangover—although she suddenly began to wonder if she *did* have a hangover after all: just didn't notice it amid her other mental agitations. Anyway, it was high time she forgot all her own troubles and involved herself with other people's.

She'd noticed Morse (and he her) as he'd walked along to the Day Room; watched him walk back, half an hour later, and spend the rest of the afternoon reading. Bookish sort of fellow, he seemed. Nice, though—and she would go and have a word with him perhaps once he put his books down. Which he didn't.

She watched him again, at 7:40 P.M., as he sat against the pillows; and more particularly watched the woman who sat beside him, in a dark-blue dress, with glints of gold and auburn in her hair, the regular small-featured face leaning forward slightly as she spoke to him. To Eileen the pair of them seemed so eager to talk to each other—so different from the conversational drought which descended on so many hospital visitations. Twice, even as she watched, the woman, in the middle of some animated little passage of dialogue, placed the tips of her fingers against the sleeve of his gaudy pyjamas, fingers that were slim and sinewy, like those of an executant musician. Eileen knew all about *that* sort of gesture! And what about him, Morse? He, too, seemed to be doing his level, unctuous best to impress *her*, with a combination of that happily manufactured half-smile and eyes that focused intently upon hers. Oh yes! She could see what each of them was feeling—nauseating couple of bootlickers! But she knew she envied them; envied especially the woman—Waggie's clever-clogs of a daughter! From the few times she'd spoken to Morse, she knew that his conversation—and perhaps, she thought, his life, too—was so *interesting*. She'd met just a few other men like that—men who were full of fascinating knowledge about architecture, history, literature, music . . . all the things after which over these last few years she'd found herself yearning. How relieved she suddenly felt that most probably her swollen-lipped forty-year-old wouldn't be able to kiss her that evening!

A man (as she now realised) had been standing patiently at the desk.

"Can I help you?"

Sergeant Lewis nodded and looked down at her. "Special instructions. I've got to report to the boss whenever I bring the Chief Inspector a bag of plastic explosive. You're the boss tonight, aren't you?"

"Don't be too hard on Sister Maclean!"

Lewis bent forward and spoke softly. "It's not me—it's him! He says she's an argumentative, bitchy old . . . old something."

Eileen smiled. "She's not very tactful, sometimes."

"He's, er—looks like he's got a visitor for the moment."

"Yes."

"Perhaps I'd better not interrupt, had I? He gets very cross sometimes."

"Does he?"

"Especially if . . ."

Eileen nodded, and looked up into Lewis's kindly face, feeling that menfolk weren't quite so bad as she'd begun to think.

"What's he like—Inspector Morse?" she asked.

Christine Greenaway stood up to go, and Morse was suddenly conscious, as she stood so closely beside the bed, how small she was—in spite of the high-heeled shoes she habitually wore. Words came back to his mind, the words he'd read again so recently: ". . . petite and attractive figure, wearing an Oxford-blue dress . . ."

"How tall are you?" asked Morse, as she smoothed her dress down over her thighs.

"How *small* am I, don't you mean?" Her eyes flashed and seemed to mock him. "In stockinged feet, I'm five feet, half an inch. And don't forget that half-inch: it may not be very important to you, but it is to me. I wear heels all the time—so I come up to about normal, usually. About five three."

"What size shoes do you take?"

"Threes. You wouldn't be able to get your feet in them."

"I've got very nice feet," said Morse seriously.

"I think I ought to be more worried about my father than about your feet," she whispered quietly, as she touched his arm once more, and as Morse in turn placed his own left hand so briefly, so lightly upon hers. It was a little moment of magic, for both of them.

"And you'll look up that—?"

"I won't forget."

Then she was gone, and only the smell of some expensive perfume lingered around the bed.

"I just wonder," said Morse, almost absently, as Lewis took Christine's place in the plastic chair, "I just wonder what size shoes Joanna Franks took. I'm assuming, of course, they *had* shoe-sizes in those days. Not a modern invention, like women's tights, are they?—shoe-sizes? What do you think, Lewis?"

"Would you like me to show you exactly what size she *did* take, sir?"

Chapter Twenty-five

Those who are incapable of committing great crimes
do not readily suspect them in others.
                    (*La Rochefoucauld,* Maxims)

Morse was invariably credited, by his police colleagues, with an alpha-plus intelligence, of a kind
which surfaced rarely on the tides of human affairs,
and which almost always gave him about six fur-
longs' start in any criminal investigation. Whatever
the truth of this matter, Morse himself knew that
one gift had never been bestowed on him—that of
reading quickly. It was to be observed, therefore,
that he seemed to spend a disproportionately long
time that evening—Christine gone, Lewis gone,
Horlicks drunk, pills swallowed, injection injected—
in reading through the photocopied columns from
Jackson's Oxford Journal. Christine had not mentioned to him that, dissatisfied with her handwritten

notes, she had returned to the Central Library in
the early afternoon and prevailed upon one of her
vague acquaintances there to let her jump the
queue and photocopy the original material directly
from their bulky originals. Not that Morse, even
had he known, would have exhibited any excessive
gratitude. One of his weaknesses was his disposi-
tion to accept loyalty without ever really understanding, certainly not appreciating, the sacrifices
that might be involved.

When, as a boy, he had been shepherded around
various archaeological sites, Morse had been unable
to share the passion of some fanatic drooling over a
few (disintegrating) Roman bricks. Even then, it had
been the written word, rather than the tangible
artefact, which had pricked his curiosity, and pro-
moted his subsequent delight in the ancient world.
It was to be expected, therefore, that although
Lewis's quite extraordinary discovery was to prove
the single most dramatic break-through in the
supposed "case," the sight of a sad-looking pair of
shrivelled shoes and an even sadder-looking pair
of crumpled knickers was, for Morse, a little anti-
climactic. At least, for the present. As for Christine's
offerings, though, how wonderfully attractive and
suggestive they were!

From the newspaper records, it was soon clear
that the Colonel had omitted no details of any obvious importance. Yet, as in most criminal cases, it

was the apparently innocuous, incidental, almost irrelevant, details that could change, in a flash, the interpretation of accepted facts. And there were quite a few details here (to Morse, hitherto unknown) which caused him more than a millimetric rise of the eyebrows.

First, reading between the somewhat smudged lines of the photocopied material, it seemed fairly clear that the charge of theft had probably been dropped at the first trial for the reason that the evidence (such as it was) had pointed predominantly to the youth, Wootton, therefore necessitating an individual prosecution—and that against a minor. If any of the other crewmen were involved, it was Towns (the man deported to Australia) who figured as the safest bet; and quite certainly no obvious evidence could be levelled against the two men eventually hanged for *murder*. What was it then that the young man's covetous eyes may have sought to steal from Joanna Franks's baggage? No answer emerged clearly from the evidence. But there was surely one thing, above all, that thieves went for, whether in 1859 or 1989: *money*.

Mmm.

Second, there was sufficient contemporary evidence to suggest that it was Joanna who was probably the sustaining partner in her second marriage. Whatever it was that had caused her to "fall deeply in love with Charles Franks, an ostler from Liverpool," it was *Joanna* who had besought her new husband to keep up his spirits during the ill fortune which had beset the early months of their marriage. An extract from a letter to Charles Franks had indeed been read out in court, presumably (as Morse saw things) to substantiate the point that, quite contrary to the boatmen's claim of *Joanna* being demented, it was *Charles* who seemed the nearer to a mental breakdown: "Sorry I am to read, my dear husband, your sadly wandering letter—do, my dear, strive against what I fear will await you should you not rest your tortured mind. The loss of reason is a terrible thing and will blight our hopes. Be strong and know we shall soon be together and well provided for." A poignant and eloquent letter.

Were *both* of them a bit unbalanced?

Mmm.

Third, various depositions from both trials made it clear that although "fly" boats worked best with a strict enforcement of a "two on—two off" arrangement, it was quite usual, in practice, for the four members of such a crew to permutate their different duties in order to accommodate individual likings or requirements. Or *desires*, perhaps? For Morse now read, with considerable interest, the evidence adduced in court (Where were you, Colonel Deniston?) that Oldfield, captain of the *Barbara Bray*, had paid Walter Towns *6d* to take over from him the arduous business of "legging" the boat through the Barton tunnel. Morse nodded to himself: for his imagination had already travelled there.

Mmm.

Fourth, the evidence, taken as a whole, suggested strongly that for the first half of the journey Joanna had joined in quite happily with the boatmen at the various stops: staying in their company, eating at the same table, drinking with them, laughing with them at their jokes. Few jokes, though, on the latter half of the journey, when, as the prosecution had pressed home again and again, Joanna figured only as a helpless, hapless soul—crying out (at times, literally) for help, sympathy, protection, mercy. And one decisive and dramatic fact: as the crew themselves grew progressively inebriated, Joanna was becoming increasingly sober; for the coroner's evidence, as reported at the trial, was incontestable: *no alcohol at all was found in her body.*

Mmm.

Morse proceeded to underline in blue Biro the various, and most curious, altercations which the law-writer of *Jackson's Oxford Journal* had deemed it worthy to record:

"Will you have anything of this?" (Oldfield) "No, I have no inclination." (Bloxham) "—'s already had his concerns with her tonight; and I will, or else I shall—her." (Oldfield) "D—n and blast the woman! If she has drowned herself, I cannot help it." (Oldfield) "She said she'd do it afore, and now she seems to 'a done it proper." (Musson) "I hope the b—y w—e is burning in hell!" (Oldfield) "Blast the woman! What do we know about her? If she had a mind to drown herself, why should we be in all this trouble?" (Towns) "If he is going to be a witness against us, it is for other things, not for the woman." (Oldfield)

Mmm.

Randomly quoted, incoherent, unchronological as they were, these extracts from the trials served most strongly to reinforce Morse's earlier conviction that they were not the sort of comments one would expect from murderers. One might expect some measure of shame, remorse, fear—yes!— even, in a few cases, triumph and jubilation in the actual performance of the deed. But not—no!— not the fierce anger and loathing perpetuated by the boatmen through the hours and the days after Joanna had met her death.

Finally, there was a further (significant?) passage of evidence which the Colonel had *not* cited. It was, apparently, Oldfield's claim that, at about 4 A.M. on the fateful morning, the boatmen *had*, in fact, caught up with Joanna—the latter in a state of much mental confusion; both he and Musson had discovered her whereabouts only by the anguished cries in which she called upon the name of her husband: "Franks! Franks! Franks!" Furthermore,

Oldfield claimed, he had actually persuaded her to get back on the boat, although he agreed that she had fairly soon jumped off again (again!) to resume her walking along the tow-path. Then, according to Oldfield, two of them, he and Towns on this occasion, had once more gone ashore, where they met another potential witness (the Donald Favant mentioned in the Colonel's book). But the boatmen had not been believed. In particular this second meeting along the tow-path had come in for withering scorn from the prosecution: at best, the confused recollection of hopelessly drunken minds; at worst, the invention of "these callous murderers." Yes! That was exactly the sort of comment which throughout had disquieted Morse's passion for justice. As a policeman, he knew only the rudiments of English Law; but he was a fervent believer in the principle that a man should be presumed innocent until he was pronounced guilty: it was a fundamental principle, not only of substantive law, but of natural justice . . .

"You comfy?" asked Eileen, automatically pulling the folds of his sheets tidy.

"I thought you'd gone off duty."

"Just going."

"You're spoiling me."

"You enjoy reading, don't you?"

Morse nodded: "Sometimes."

"You like reading best of all?"

"Well, music—music, I suppose, sometimes more."

"So, if you're reading a book with the record-player going—"

"I can't enjoy them both together."

"But they're the *best*?"

"Apart from a candle-lit evening-meal with some-one like you."

Eileen coloured, her pale cheeks suddenly as bright as those of the dying Colonel.

Before going to sleep that night, Morse's hand glided into the bedside cabinet and poured out a small measure; and as he sipped the Scotch, at his own pace, the world of a sudden was none too bad a place . . .

When he awoke (was awoken, rather) the follow-ing morning (Sunday) he marvelled that the blind-ingly obvious notion that now occurred to him had taken such an age to materialise. Usually, his cere-bral analysis was as swift as the proverbial snap of a lizard's eyelid.

Or so he told himself.

Chapter Twenty-six

> Now, there is a law written in the darkest of the Books
> of Life, and it is this: If you look at a thing nine hun-
> dred and ninety-nine times, you are perfectly safe; if
> you look at it for the thousandth time, you are in
> frightful danger of seeing it for the first time.
> (*G. K. Chesterton,* The Napoleon of Notting Hill)

Just the same with crosswords puzzles, wasn't it?
Sit and ponder more and more deeply over some
abstruse clue—and get nowhere. Stand away,
though—further back!—further back still!—and
the answer will shout at you with a sort of mocking
triumph. It was those shoes, of course . . . shoes at
which he'd been staring so hard he hadn't really
seen them.

Morse waited with keen anticipation until his morning ablutions were complete before re-re-reading
the Colonel's work, lingering over things—as he'd

always done as a boy when he'd carved his way meticulously around the egg-white until he was left only with the golden circle of the yolk, into which, finally, to dip the calculated balance of his chips.

What were the actual words of the trial report? Yes, Morse nodded to himself: when Charles Franks had looked at the body, he had recognised it, dreadfully disfigured as it was, by "a small mark behind his wife's left ear, a mark of which only a parent or an intimate lover could have known." *Or a scoundrel.* By all the gods, was *ever* identification so tenuously asserted and attested in the English Courts? Not only some tiny disfigurement in a place where no one else would have been aware of it, but a tiny disfigurement which existed *on* the head of Joanna Franks only because it existed *in* the head of her new husband! Oh, it must have been there all right! The doctor, the coroner, the inspector of police, those who'd undressed the dead woman, and redressed her for a proper Christian burial—so many witnesses who could, if need ever arose, corroborate the existence of such a blemish on what had once been such a pretty face. But who could, or did, corroborate the fact that the face had been *Joanna*'s? The husband? Yes, he'd had his say. But the only others who might have known, the parents—where were they? Apparently, they'd played no part at all in the boatmen's trial at Oxford. Why not? Was the mother too stricken with grief to give any coherent testimony? Was she *alive*, even, at the time of the trial? The father was alive, though, wasn't he? The insurance man . . .

Morse brought his mind back to the central point he was seeking to establish before his own imagined jury (little "j"). No court would have accepted such unilateral identification without *something* to support it—and there *had* been something (again Morse looked back to the actual words): corroboration was afforded "by the shoes, later found in the fore-cabin of the *Barbara Bray*, which matched in the minutest degrees the contours of the dead woman's feet." So, the matter was clear: one, the shoes in the cabin belonged to Joanna Franks; two, the shoes had been worn by the drowned woman; therefore, three, the drowned woman was Joanna Franks—QED. Even Aristotle might have been satisfied with such a syllogism. Incontrovertible! All three statements as true as the Eternal Verities; and if so, the shoes *must* belong to the woman who was drowned. But . . . but what if the first statement was *not* true? What if the shoes had *not* belonged to Joanna? Then the inexorable conclusion must be that whatever was found floating face-downward at Duke's Cut in 1859, *it was not the body of Joanna Franks.*

Just one moment, Morse!! (The voice of the prosecution was deafening against his ear.) All right! The identification as it stood, as it stands, may perchance appear a trifle tenuous? But have you—*you*—any—*any*—reason for discrediting such identification? And the answering voice in Morse's brain—*Morse's* voice—was firm and confident. Indeed! And if it should please my learned friends I shall now proceed to tell you exactly what *did* happen between 3 A.M. and 5 A.M. on the morning of Wednesday, the 22nd June, in 1859.

Gentlemen! We who are engaged in seeking to reconstruct the course as well as the causation of crime are often tormented by the same insistent thought: *something* must have happened, and happened *in a specific way*. All theory, all reconstruction, all probability, are as nothing compared with *the simple, physical truth of what actually happened at the time.* If only . . . if only, we say, we could see it all; see it all as it actually happened! Gentlemen, I am about to tell you—

Proceed! said the judge (little "j").

Chapter Twenty-seven

> Imagination, that dost so abstract us
> That we are not aware, not even when
> A thousand trumpets sound about our ears!
> (*Dante*, Purgatorio)

Standing by the door at the left of the fore-cabin, she could see them both. A reporter, perhaps, would have had them dribbling or vomiting; snoring "stertorously," certainly. But Joanna was to notice, at that point, only the simple fact, the undramatic circumstance: asleep, the pair of them—Oldfield and Musson—only the slight rise and fall of the faded maroon eiderdown that covered them both betraying their fitful breathing. Drunk? Yes, *very* drunk: but Joanna herself had seen to that. Little or no persuasion required—but the *timing* important . . . She smiled grimly to herself, and consulted the little silver time-piece she always kept so carefully about her person: the watch her father had given her on her twenty-second birthday (not her twenty-first)—when some fees had been forthcoming from the London Patent Office. And again, now, her hand closed around the precious watch as if it were a talisman for the success of the imminent enterprise.

Occasionally she spoke quietly—very quietly—to the shifty, silly, spotty-faced youth who stood beside her at the entrance to the cabin: his left hand upon the Z-shaped tiller, painted in alternate bands of red, green, yellow; his right hand (where she had placed it herself!) fondling the bosom of her dress. Twenty-five yards ahead, the horse (rather a good one!) was plodding along a little more slowly now, the wooden bobbins stretched taut along its flanks as it forged forward along the silent tow-path—with only the occasional flap of the waters heard as they slurped against the *Barbara Bray*, heading ever southwards into the night.

Joanna looked briefly behind her now, at the plaited basket-work that protected the narrow-boat's stern. "Over a bit *more*, Tom!" she whispered, as the boat moved into the elbow-bend at Thrupp, just past the village of Hampton Gay. "And don't forget our little bargain," she added as she stepped up on to the side, whilst Wootton gently manoeuvred the boat ever closer in towards the right-hand bank.

Wootton would not be celebrating his fifteenth

birthday until the February of 1860, but already, in several ways, he was a good deal older than his years. Not in *every* way, though. Never, before Joanna had come on board at Preston Brook, had he felt so besotted with a woman as he was with *her*. Exactly, as he knew, the rest of the crew had been. There was something sexually animated, and *compelling*, about Joanna Franks. Something about the way she flashed her eyes when she spoke; something about the way her tongue lightly licked the corners of her mouth after a plate of muttonchops and peas at some low-roofed tavern alongside the canal; something wickedly and calculatedly controlled about her, as she'd drunk her own full share of liquor—that happily awaited, worry-effacing liquor that all the boatmen (including Wootton) drank so regularly along their journeys. *And Oldfield had taken possession of her*—of that Wootton was quite sure! Taken her in one of the pitch-black transit-tunnels when he, Wootton, had gladly taken Oldfield's 6*d*, and "legged" the *Barbara Bray* slowly towards that pin-point of light which had gradually grown ever larger as darkly he'd listened to the strangely exciting noises of the love-making taking place in the bunk below him. Towns, too, had taken Oldfield's 6*d* in a tunnel further south. And both Towns and Musson—the lanky, lecherous-eyed Musson!—knew only too well what was going on, soon wanting a share of things for themselves.

No surprise, then, that nasty incident when Towns had gone for Musson—with a knife!

As agreed, Thomas Wootton provided her with the lantern. The night, though dark, was dry and still; and the flame nodded only spasmodically as she took it, and leaped lightly off the *Barbara Bray*—her bonnet around her head, her shoes on her feet—on to the tow-path bank where, very soon, she had disappeared from the youth who now kept looking straight ahead of him, a smile around his wide, lascivious mouth.

It was not unusual, of course, for women passengers to jump ashore at fairly regular intervals from a narrow-boat: female toiletry demanded a greater measure of decorum than did that for men. But Joanna might be gone a little longer than was usual that night . . . so she'd said.

She stood back in the undergrowth, watching the configuration of the boat melt deeper and deeper into the night. Then, gauging she was out of earshot of the crew, she called out the man's name— without at first receiving a reply: then again; then a third time—until she heard a rustling movement in the bushes beside her, against the stone wall of a large mansion house—and a suppressed, tense, "Shsh!"

The night air was very still, and her voice had carried far too clearly down the canal, with both the youth at the helm, and the man with the stoical horse, turning round simultaneously to look into the dark. But they could see nothing; and *hearing* nothing further, neither of them was giving the matter much further thought.

But one of the men supposedly asleep had heard it, too!

Meanwhile Joanna and her accomplice had flitted stealthily along the row of small, grey-stoned, terraced cottages which lined the canal at Thrupp, keeping to the shadows; then, gliding unobserved past the darkened, silent windows of the Boat Inn, they moved, more freely now, along the short hedge-lined lane that led to the Oxford-Banbury highway.

For the *Barbara Bray*, the next three miles of the Oxford Canal would interpose the Roundham, Kidlington Green, and Shuttleworth's locks—the latter just north of the basin of water known as Duke's Cut. Negotiation of these locks (so carefully calculated!) would afford appropriate opportunity. No real problem. Much more difficult had been the arrangements of meeting each other; and certainly Oldfield, more than once, had looked at Joanna suspiciously in the last twenty-four hours as she had taken (but of necessity!) her diurnal and nocturnal promenades. She knew, though, how to deal with Oldfield, the skipper of the *Barbara Bray* ...

* * *

"Everything ready?"

He nodded, brusquely. "Don't talk now!"

They walked across to a covered carrier's wagon which stood, a piebald horse between its shafts, tethered to a beech tree just beside the verge. The moon appeared fitfully from behind the slow-moving cloud; not a soul was in sight.

"Knife?" he asked.

"I sharpened it."

He nodded with a cruel satisfaction.

She took off her cloak and handed it to him; taking, in return, the one he passed to her—similar to her own, though cheaper in both cloth and cut, and slightly longer.

"You didn't forget the handkerchief?"

Quickly she re-checked, drawing from the right-hand pocket of her former cloak the small, white square of linen, trimmed with lace, the initials J.F. worked neatly in pink silk in one corner.

Clever touch!

"She's—she's in there?" Joanna half-turned to the back of the wagon, for the first time her voice sounding nervous, though unexpectedly harsh.

He jerked his head, once, his small eyes bright in the heavily bearded face.

"I don't really want to see her."

"No need!" He had taken the lantern; and when the two of them had climbed up to the front of the wagon, he shone it on a hand-drawn map, his right forefinger pointing to a bridge over the canal, some four hundred yards north of Shuttleworth's Lock. "We go down to—here! You wait there, and catch up with them, all right? Then get on board again. Then after that—*after* you get through the lock— you . . ."

"What we agreed!"

"Yes. Jump in! You can stay in the water as long as you like. But be sure no one sees you getting out! The wagon'll be next to the bridge. You get in! And lie still! All right? I'll be there as soon as I've . . ."

Joanna took the knife from her skirt. "Do you want *me* to do it?"

"No!" He took the knife quickly.

"No?"

"It's just," he resumed, "that her face, well—well, it's gone *black*!"

"I thought dead people usually went white," whispered Joanna.

The man climbed on to the fore-board, and helped her up, before disappearing briefly into the darkness of the covered cart; where, holding the lantern well away from the face, he lifted the dead woman's skirts and with the skill of a surgeon made an incision of about five or six inches down the front of her calico knickers.

The man was handing Joanna two bottles of dark-looking "Running Horse" ale, when he felt the firm grip of her hand on his shoulder, shaking, shaking, shaking . . .

"Some soup for you, Mr. Morse?"

It was Violet.

(Not the soup.)

Chapter Twenty-eight

> Mendacity is a system that we live in. Liquor is one
> way out and death's the other.
> (*Tennessee Williams,* Cat on a Hot Tin Roof)

The "Report" was a regular feature of all the wards
in the JR2, comprising a meeting of hospital and
medical staff at the change-over points between
the Early, Late, and Night shifts. In several of the
wards, the weekends offered the chance for some
top consultants and other senior medical personnel
to concentrate their attention on such sidelines
as boating and BMWs. But in many of the semi-
surgical wards, like Ward 7C, the Reports went on
very much as at any other times; as they did on
what was now the second Sunday of Morse's stay in
hospital.

The 1 P.M. meeting that day was, in fact, well attended: the Senior Consultant, a junior houseman,

Sister Maclean, Charge Nurse Stanton, and two student nurses. Crowded into Sister's small office, the group methodically appraised the patients in the ward, briefly discussing convalescences, relapses, prognoses, medications, and associated problems.

Morse, it appeared, was no longer much of a problem.

"Morse!" The hint of a smile could be observed on the Consultant's face as he was handed the relevant notes.

"He's making fairly good progress," Sister asserted, slightly defensively, like some mother at a Parents' Evening hearing that her child was perhaps not working as hard as he should be.

"Some of us," confided the Consultant (handing back the notes) "would like to persuade these dedicated drinkers that water is a wonderful thing. I wouldn't try to persuade you, of course, Sister, but . . ."

For a minute or two Sister Maclean's pale cheeks were flooded with bright-pink suffusion, and one of the student nurses could barely suppress a smile of delight at the Dragon's discomfiture. But oddly, the other of the two, the Fair Fiona, was suddenly aware of lineaments and colouring in Sister's face that could have made it almost beautiful.

"He doesn't seem to drink *that* much, does he?" suggested the young houseman, his eyes skimming the plentiful notes, several of which he had composed himself.

The Consultant snorted contemptuously: "Nonsense!" He flicked his finger at the offending sheets. "Bloody liar, isn't he? Drunkards and diabetics!"—he turned to the houseman—"I've told you that before, I think?"

It was wholly forgivable that for a few seconds the suspicion of a smile hovered around the lips of Sister Maclean, her cheeks now restored to their wonted palidity.

"He's not diabetic—" began the houseman.

"Give him a couple of years!"

"He *is* on the mend, though." The houseman (and rightly!) was determined to claim *some* small credit for the reasonably satisfactory transit of Chief Inspector Morse through the NHS.

"Bloody lucky! Even I was thinking about cutting half his innards away!"

"He must be a fundamentally strong sort of man," admitted Sister, composure now fully recovered.

"I suppose so," conceded the Consultant, "apart from his stomach, his lungs, his kidneys, his liver—especially his liver. He might last till he's sixty if he does what we tell him—which I doubt."

"Keep him another few days, you think?"

"No!" decided the Consultant, after a pause. "No! Send him home! His wife'll probably do just as good a job as we can. Same medication—out-patients' in two weeks—to see *me*. OK?"

Eileen Stanton was about to correct the Consultant on his factual error when a nurse burst into the office. "I'm sorry, Sister—but there's a cardiac arrest, I think—in one of the Amenity Beds."

"Did he die?" asked Morse.

Eileen, who had come to sit on his bed, nodded sadly. It was mid-afternoon.

"How old was he?"

"Don't know exactly. Few years younger than you, I should think." Her face was glum. "Perhaps if . . ."

"You look as you could do with a bit of tender loving care yourself," said Morse, reading her thoughts.

"Yes!" She looked at him and smiled, determined to snap out of her mopishness. "And *you*, my good sir, are not going to get very much more of our wonderful loving care—after today. We're kicking you out tomorrow—had quite enough of you!"

"I'm going out, you mean?" Morse wasn't sure if it was good news or bad news; but she told him.

"Good news, isn't it?"

"I shall miss you."

"Yes, I shall . . ." But Morse could see the tears welling up in her eyes.

"Why don't you tell me what's wrong?" He

spoke the words softly; and she told him. Told him about her wretched week; and how kind the hospital had been in letting her switch her normal nights; and how kind, especially, *Sister* had been ... But the big tears were rolling down her cheeks and she turned away and held one hand to her face, searching with the other for her handkerchief. Morse put his own grubby handkerchief gently into her hand, and for a moment the two sat together in silence.

"I'll tell you one thing," said Morse at last. "It must be pretty flattering to have a couple of fellows fighting over you."

"No! No, it *isn't*!" The tears were forming again in the large, sad eyes.

"No! You're right. But listen! It won't do you any good at all—in fact" (Morse whispered) "it'll make you feel far worse. But if *I'd* been at that party of yours—when they were fighting over you—I'd have taken on the *pair* of 'em! You'd have had *three* men squabbling over you—not just two."

She smiled through her tears, and wiped her wet cheeks, already feeling much better. "They're big men, both of them. One of them takes lessons in some of those Martial Arts."

"All right—I'd've lost! Still have fought for you, though, wouldn't I? Remember the words of the poet? 'Better to have fought and lost than ... something ... something ...' " (Morse himself had apparently *forgotten* the words of the poet.)

She brought her face to within a few inches of his, and looked straight into his eyes: "I wouldn't have minded a little bit if you *had* lost, providing you'd let me look after you."

"You *have* been looking after me," said Morse, "and thank you!"

Getting to her feet, she said no more. And Morse, with a little wistfulness, watched her as she walked away. Perhaps he should have told her that she'd meant "provided," not "providing"? No! Such things, Morse knew, were no great worry to the majority of his fellow men and women.

But they were to him.

Chapter Twenty-nine

> I think it frets the saints in heaven to see
> How many desolate creatures on the earth
> Have learnt the simple dues of fellowship
> And social comfort, in a hospital.
> (*Elizabeth Barrett Browning*,
> Aurora Leigh)

There is a sadness which invariably and mysteriously accompanies the conclusion of any journey, and the end of any sojourn. Whether or not such sadness is a presage of the last journey we all must take; whether or not it is, more simply, a series of last, protracted goodbyes—it is not of any import here to speculate. But for Morse, the news that he was forthwith to be discharged from the JR2 was simultaneously wonderful—and woeful. Music awaited him? Indeed! Soon he would be luxuriating again in Wotan's Farewell from the last act of *Die Walküre;* and turning up Pavarotti *fff* from one

207

of the Puccinis—certainly in mid-morning, when his immediate neighbours were always out and about on their good works for Oxfam. Books, too. He trusted that the Neighbourhood Watch had done its duty in North Oxford, and that his first edition of *A Shropshire Lad* (1896) was still in its place on his shelves, that slim, white volume that stood proudly amongst its fellows, carrying no extra insurance-cover, like a Royal Prince without a personal bodyguard. Yes, it would be good to get home again: to please himself about what he listened to, or read, or ate . . . or drank. Well, within reason. Yet, quite certainly, he would miss the hospital! Miss the nurses, miss the fellow-patients, miss the routine, miss the visitors—miss so much about the institution which, with its few faults and its many virtues, had admitted him in his sickness and was now discharging him in a comparative health.

But the departure from Ward 7C was not, for Morse, to be a memorable experience. When the message came—hardly a bugle-call!—to join a group of people who were to be ambulanced up to North Oxford, he had little opportunity of saying farewell to anyone. One of his wardmates ("Waggie") was performing his first post-operatively independent ablutions in the washroom; another was very fast asleep; one had just been taken to the X-ray Department; the Ethiopian torch-bearer was sitting in his bed, with Do-Not-Disturb written all

over him, reading *The Blue Ticket* (!); and the last
was (and had been for hours) closeted behind his
curtains, clearly destined little longer for this
earthly life; perhaps, indeed, having already said
his own farewells to everybody. As for the nurses,
most were bustling purposively about their duties
(one or two new faces, anyway), and Morse real-
ized that he was just another patient, and one no
longer requiring that special care of just one week
ago. Eileen he had not expected to see again, now
back to her normal Nights, as she'd told him. Nor
was Sister herself anywhere to be seen as he was
wheeled out of the ward by a cheerful young porter
with a crew-cut and earrings. The Fair Fiona,
though, he did see—sitting patiently in the next bay
beside an ancient citizen, holding a sputum-pot in
front of his dribbling lips. With her free hand she
waved, and mouthed a "Good luck!" But Morse
was no lip-reader and, uncomprehending, he was
pushed on through the exit corridor where he and
his attendant waited for the service-lift to arrive at
Level 7.

Chapter Thirty

> *Lente currite, noctis equi!*
> (Oh gallop slow, you horses of the night!)
> (*Ovid*, Amores)

Although Mrs. Green had kept Morse's partial central-heating partially on, the flat seemed cold and unwelcoming. It would have been good for *anyone* to be there to welcome him: certainly (and especially) Christine—or Eileen, or Fiona; even, come to think of it, the dreaded Dragon of the Loch herself. But there was no one. Lewis had not been in to clear up the stuff stuck through the letter-box, and Morse picked up two white-enveloped Christmas cards (one from his insurance company, with the facsimiled signature of the managing director); and his two Sunday newspapers. Such newspapers, although there was an occasional permutation of titles, invariably reflected the conflict in Morse's mind between the Cultured and the Coarse—the choice between the front page of the present one, SYNOD IN DISPUTE OVER DISESTAB-LISHMENT, and SEX SLAVE'S SIX-WEEK ORDEAL IN SILK-LINED COFFIN of the other. If Morse chose the latter first (as, in fact, he did) at least he had the excuse that it was undoubtedly the finer headline. And this Sunday, as usual, he first flicked through the pages of full-breasted photographs and features on Hollywood intrigues and Soap infidelities. Then, he made himself a cup of instant coffee (which he much preferred to "the real thing") before settling down to read about the most recent fluctuations on the world's stock-markets, and the bleak prospects for the diseased and starving millions of the world's unhappy continents.

At half-past five the phone rang, and Morse knew that if he had one wish only it would be for the caller to be Christine.

The caller was Christine.

Not only had she located the rare (and extraordinarily valuable) book of which Morse had enquired, but she had spent an hour or so that afternoon ("Don't tell anyone!") reading through the relevant pages, and discovering ("Don't be disappointed!") that only one short chapter was given over to the interview, between Samuel Carter and an ageing Walter Towns, concerning the trial of the boatmen.

"That's wonderful!" said Morse. "Where are you ringing from?"

"From, er, from home." (Why the hesitation?)

"Perhaps—"

"Look!" she interrupted. "I've made a photo-copy. Would you like me to send it through the post? Or I could—"

"Could you read it quickly over the phone? It's fairly short, you say?"

"I'm not a very good reader."

"Put the phone down—and I'll ring you back! Then we can talk as long as we like."

"I'm not as hard up as all *that*, you know."

"All right—fire away!"

"Page 187, it begins—ready?"

"Ready, miss!"

Of the persons encountered in Perth in these last months of 1884 was a man called Walter Towns. Although he was known as a local celebrity, I found it difficult to guess the quality which had avowedly brought such renown to the rather—nay, wholly!—miserable specimen to whom I soon was introduced. He was a small man, of only some five feet in stature, thin, and of a gaunt mien, with deeply furrowed creases down each of his cheeks from eye to mouth; further-more, his exceedingly sallow complexion had re-mained untouched by the rays of a sun that is powerful in this region, and his hollow aspect was further enhanced by the complete absence of teeth in the upper jaw. Yet his eyes spoke a latent (if limited) intelligence; and also a certain dolefulness, as if he were remembering things done long ago and things done ill. In truth, the situation pertaining to this man was fully as melodramatic as my readers could have wished; for he had been reprieved from the gallows with minutes only to spare. It was with the utmost interest and curiosity, therefore, that I questioned him.

A woman had been murdered near Oxford in 1860, on the local canal, and suspicion had centered on the crew of a narrow-boat plying south towards London. The four members of the crew, including both Towns himself and a lad of some fourteen years, had duly been arrested and brought to Court. Whilst the youth had been acquitted, the three others had been convicted, and incarcerated in the gaol in the city of Oxford, awaiting public execution. It was here, two or three minutes following the final visit of the Court Chaplain to the prisoners in their condemned cells, that Towns had received the news of his reprieve. Few humans, certainly can have experienced a peripeteia [Christine here reverted to the spelling] so dramatic to their fortunes. Yet my conversation with Towns proved a matter of some considerable disappointment. Barely literate as the man was (though wholly understandably so) he was also barely comprehensible. His West Country dialect (as I straightaway placed it) was to such an extent o'erlaid with the excesses of the Australian manner of speech that I could follow some of his statements only with great difficulty. In short, the man I now met seemed ill-equipped to cope with the rigours of life—certainly those demanded of a free man. And Towns *was* a "free" man, after serving his fifteen years' penal servitude in the Longbay Penitentiary. A broken, witless man; a man old before his time (he was but 47), a veteran convict (or "crawler") who had experienced the ineffable agonies of a man faced with execution on the morrow.

Concerning the gruesome and macabre events invariably associated with the final hours of such criminals, I could learn but little. Yet a few facts may be of interest to my readers. It is clear, for example, that the prisoners each breakfasted on roasted lamb, with vegetables, although it seems probable from Towns' hazy recollection that such or similar breakfasts had been available during the whole period following the fixing of the date for their execution. More distressing, from Towns' viewpoint, was being denied access to his fellow criminals; and if

I understood the unfortunate man aright it was this "deprivation" which had been the hardest thing for him to bear. Whether he had slept little or not at all during the fateful night, Towns could not well remember; nor whether he had prayed for forgiveness and deliverance. But a miracle had occurred!

Surprisingly, it had not been the hanging itself which had been the focal-point of Towns' tortured thoughts that night. Rather it had been the knowledge of the public interest aroused in the case—the notoriety, the infamy, the horror, the abomination, the grisly spectacle, *the fame;* a fame which might bring those hapless men to walk the last few, fatal yards with a degree of fortitude which even the most pitiless spectators could admire.

Of the crime itself, Towns protested his complete innocence—a protestation not without precedent in criminal archives! But his recollection of the canal journey—and especially of the victim herself, Joanna Franks—was vivid and most poignant. The woman had been, in Towns' eyes, quite wondrously attractive, and it may cause no surprise that she became, almost immediately, the object of the men's craving, and the cause of open jealousies. Indeed, Towns recalled an occasion when two of the crew (the two who were eventually hanged) had come to blows over that provocative and desirable woman. And one of them with a knife! Even the young boy, Harold Wootton, had come under her spell, and the older woman had without much doubt taken advantage of his infatuation. At the same time, from what Towns asserted, and from the manner of his assertion, I am of the view that he himself did not have sexual dealings with the woman.

There is one interesting addendum to be made. In the first indictment (as I have subsequently read) the charge of either rape or theft would possibly have been prosecuted with more success than that of murder. Yet it was to be the charge of murder that was brought in the second trial. In similar instances, we may observe that the minor charge will frequently be suppressed when the major charge appears the more likely to be sustained. Was this, then, the reason why Towns seemed comparatively loquacious about the suggestion of *theft*? I know not. But it was his belief, as recounted to me, that Wootton had rather more interest in theft than in rape. After all, the availability of sexual dealings in 1860 was hardly, as now, a rarity along the English canals.

"Well, that's it! I'll put it in the post tonight, so you should—"

"Can't you call round, and bring it?"

"Life's, well, it's just a bit hectic at the minute," she replied, after a little, awkward silence.

"All right!" Morse needed no further excuses. Having dipped the thermometer into the water, he'd found the reading a little too cold for any prospect of mixed bathing.

"You see," said Christine, "I—I'm living with someone—"

"And he doesn't think you should go spending all your time helping me."

"I kept talking about you, too," she said quietly.

Morse said nothing.

"Is your address the same as in the telephone directory? E. Morse?"

"That's me! That is I, if you prefer it."

"What does the 'E' stand for? I never knew what to call you."

"They just call me 'Morse.' "

"You won't forget me?" she asked, after a little pause.

"I'll try to, I suppose."

Morse thought of her for many minutes after he had cradled the phone. Then he recalled the testimony of Samuel Carter, and marvelled that a researcher of Carter's undoubted experience and integrity could make so many factual errors in the course of three or four pages: the date of the murder; Towns's accent; Towns's age; Wootton's Christian name; the dropping of the rape charge . . . Very interesting, though. Why, Morse had even guessed right about that dust-up with the knife! Well, almost right: he'd got the wrong man, but . . .

Chapter Thirty-one

> The second coastline is turned towards Spain and the west, and off it lies the island of Hibernia, which according to estimates is only half the size of Britain.
>
> *(Julius Caesar, de Bello Gallico—*
> *on the geography of Ireland)*

Ten minutes later the phone rang again, and Morse knew in his bones that it was Christine Greenaway.

It was Strange.

"You're out then, Morse—yes? That's good. You've had a bit of a rough ride, they tell me."

"On the mend now, sir. Kind of you to ring."

"No *great* rush, you know—about getting back, I mean. We're a bit understaffed at the minute, but give yourself a few days—to get over things. Delicate thing, the stomach, you know. Why don't you try to get away somewhere for a couple of days—new surroundings—four-star hotel? You can afford it, Morse."

"Thank you, sir. By the way, they've signed me off for a fortnight—at the hospital."

"Fortnight? A *fort*-night?"

"It's, er, a delicate thing, the stomach, sir."

"Yes, well . . ."

"I'll be back as soon as I can, sir. And perhaps it wouldn't do me any harm to take your advice— about getting away for a little while."

"Do you a world of good! The wife's brother" (Morse groaned inwardly) "he's just back from a wonderful holiday. Ireland—Southern Ireland— took the car—Fishguard—Dun Laoghaire—then the west coast—you know, Cork, Kerry, Killarney, Connemara—marvelous, he said. Said you couldn't have spotted a terrorist with a telescope!"

It *had* been kind of Strange to ring; and as he sat in his armchair Morse reached idly for the World Atlas from his "large-book" shelf, in which Ireland was a lozenge shape of green and yellow on page 10—a country which Morse had never really contemplated before. Although spelling errors would invariably provoke his wrath, he confessed to himself that he could never have managed "Dun Laoghaire," even with a score of attempts. And where was Kerry? Ah yes! Over there, west of Tralee—he was on the right bit of the map—and he moved his finger up the coast to Galway Bay. Then he saw it: *Bertnaghboy Bay!* And suddenly the thought of going over to Connemara seemed over-whelmingly attractive. By himself? Yes, it probably had to be by himself; and he didn't mind that, really. He was somewhat of a loner by temperament—because though never wholly happy when alone he was usually slightly more miserable when with other people. It would have been good to have taken Christine, but . . . and for a few minutes Morse's thoughts travelled back to Ward 7C. He would send a card to Eileen and Fiona; and one to "Waggie" Greenaway, perhaps? Yes, that would be a nice gesture: Waggie had been out in the wash-room when Morse had left, and he'd been a pleasant old—

Suddenly Morse was conscious of the tingling excitement in the nape of his neck, and then in his shoulders. His eyes dilated and sparkled as if some inner current had been activated; and he sat back in the armchair and smiled slowly to himself.

What, he wondered, was the routine in the Irish Republic for *exhumation*?

Chapter Thirty-two

> Oh what a tangled web we weave
> When first we practise to deceive!
> (*Sir Walter Scott,* Marmion)

"You *what*?" asked a flabbergasted Lewis, who had called round at 7:30 P.M. ("Not till *The Archers* has finished" had been his strict instruction.) He himself had made an interesting little discovery—well, the WPC in St. Aldates' had made it, really—and he was hoping that it might amuse Morse in his wholly inconsequential game of "Find Joanna Franks." But to witness Morse galloping ahead of the Hunt, chasing (as Lewis was fairly certain) after some imaginary fox of his own, was, if not particularly unusual, just a little disconcerting.

"You see, Lewis" (Morse was straightway in full swing) "this is one of the most beautiful little deceptions we've ever come across. The *problems* inherent

225

in the case—almost all of them—are resolved immediately once we take one further step into imaginative improbability."

"You've lost me already, sir," protested Lewis.

"No, I haven't! Just take one more step *yourself.* You think you're in the *dark*? Right? But the dark is where we *all* are. The dark is where *I* was, until I took one more step into the dark. And then, when I'd taken it, I found myself in the *sunshine*."

"I'm very glad to hear it," mumbled Lewis.

"It's like this. Once I read that story, I was uneasy about it—doubtful, uncomfortable. It was the *identification* bit that worried me—and it would have worried any officer in the Force today, *you* know that! But, more significantly, if we consider the psychology of the whole—"

"Sir!" (It was almost unprecedented for Lewis to interrupt the Chief in such peremptory fashion.) "Could we—could you—please forget all this psychological referencing? I just about get my fill of it all from some of these Social Services people. Could you just tell me, simply and—"

"I'm boring you—is that what you're saying?"

"*Exactly* what I'm saying, sir."

Morse nodded to himself happily. "Let's put it *simply*, then, all right? I read a story in hospital. I get interested. I think—*think*—the wrong people got arrested, and some of 'em hanged, for the murder of that little tart from Liverpool. As I say, I thought the identification of that lady was a bit questionable; and when I read the words the boatmen were alleged to have used about her—well, I knew there must be something fundamentally *wrong*. You see—"

"You said you'd get to the point, sir."

"I thought that Joanna's father—No! Let's start again! Joanna's father gets a job as an insurance rep. Like most people in that position he gets a few of his own family, if they're daft enough, to take out a policy with him. He gets a bit of commission, and he's not selling a phoney product, anyway, is he? I think that both Joanna and her *first* husband, our conjurer friend, were soon enlisted in the ranks of the policy-holders. Then times get tough; and to crown all the misfortunes, Mr. Donavan, the greatest man in all the world, goes and dies. And when Joanna's natural grief has abated—or evaporated, rather—she finds she's done very-nicely-thank-you out of the insurance taken on his life. She receives £100, with profits, on what had been a policy taken out only two or three years previously. Now, £100 plus in 1850-whenever was a very considerable sum of money; and Joanna perhaps began, at that point, to appreciate the potential for *malpractice* in the system. She began to see the insurance business not only as a potential *future* benefit, but as an actual, *present* source of profit. So, after Donavan's death, when she met and married Franks, one of the first things she insisted on was his taking out a policy—not on *his* life—but on *hers*. Her father could, and did, effect such a transaction without any trouble, although it was probably soon after this that the Notts and Midlands Friendly Society got a *little* suspicious about Joanna's father, Carrick—Daniel Carrick—and told him his services were no longer—"

"Sir!"

Morse held up his right hand. "Joanna Franks was *never* murdered, Lewis! She was the mastermind—mistressmind—behind a deception that was going to rake in some considerable, and desperately needed, profit. It was *another* woman, roughly the same age and the same height, who was found in the Oxford Canal; a woman provided by Joanna's *second* husband, the ostler from the Edgware Road, who had already made his journey—not difficult for *him*!—with horse and carriage from London, to join his wife at Oxford. Or, to be more accurate, Lewis, at some few points *north* of Oxford. You remember in the Colonel's book?" (Morse turned to the passage he had in mind.) "He—here it is!— 'he explained how in consequence of some information he had come into Oxfordshire'—Bloody liar!"

Lewis, now interested despite himself, nodded a vague concurrence of thought. "So what you're saying, sir, is that Joanna worked this insurance fiddle and probably made quite a nice little packet for herself and her father as well?"

"Yes! But not only that. Listen! I may just be wrong, Lewis, but I think that not only was Joanna wrongly identified as the lawful wife of Charles Franks—by Charles Franks—but that Charles Franks was the *only* husband of the woman supposedly murdered on the *Barbara Bray*. In short, the 'Charles Franks' who broke down in tears at the second trial was *none other than Donavan*."

"Phew!"

"A man of many parts: he was an actor, he was a conjurer, he was an impersonator, he was a swindler, he was a cunning schemer, he was a callous murderer, he was a loving husband, he was a tearful witness, he was the first and *only* husband of Joanna Franks: F. T. Donavan! We all thought—you thought—even *I* thought—that there were three principal characters playing their rôles in our little drama; and now I'm telling you, Lewis, that in all probability we've only got *two*. Joanna; and her husband—the greatest man in all the world; the man buried out on the west coast of Ireland, where the breakers come rolling in from the Atlantic ... so they tell me ...

Chapter Thirty-three

Lewis was silent. How else? He had a precious little piece of evidence in his pocket, but while Morse's mind was still coursing through the upper atmosphere, there was little point in interrupting again for the minute. He put the envelope containing the single photocopied sheet on the coffee table—and listened further.

"In the account of Joanna's last few days, we've got some evidence that she could have been a bit deranged; and part of the evidence for such a possibility is the fact that at some point she kept calling out her husband's name—'Franks! Franks! Franks!' Agreed? But she *wasn't* calling out that at all—she was calling her *first* husband, Lewis! I was sitting here thinking of 'Waggie' Greenaway—"

"And his daughter," mumbled Lewis, inaudibly.

"—and I thought of 'Hefty' Donavan. F.T. Donavan. And I'll put my next month's salary on that 'F' standing for 'Frank'! Huh! Who's ever heard of a wife calling her husband by his surname?"

"I have, sir."

"Nonsense! Not these days."

"But it's *not* these days. It was—"

"She was calling *Frank Donavan*—believe me!"

"But she *could* have been queer in the head, and if so—"

"Nonsense!"

"Well, we shan't ever know for sure, shall we, sir?"

"Nonsense!"

Morse sat back with the self-satisfied, authoritative air of a man who believes that what he has called "nonsense" three times must, by the laws of the universe, be necessarily untrue. "If *only* we knew how tall they were—Joanna and . . . and whoever the other woman was. But there *is* just a chance, isn't there? That cemetery, Lewis—"

"Which do you want first, sir? The good news or the bad news?"

Morse frowned at him. "That's . . . ?" pointing to the envelope.

"That's the good news."

Morse slowly withdrew and studied the photocopied sheet.

> Twenty five minutes past 7 o'clock.
> Drowned body was in cut
> of wk licensed to B of M —
> taken to Plough Inn at Wolv —
> probable identity? unknown.
> Prelim findings wd suggest
> death by drowning — no obvious
> injury was seen — 5 3¾ in —
> well nour — c 35 yrs. Bruise
> on mouth (rt side) — body warm
> full clothes, _not_ bonnet &
> shoes — face discoloured, black.

"Not the Coroner's Report, sir, but the next best thing. This fellow must have seen her before the *post-mortem*. Interesting, isn't it?"

"*Very* interesting."

The report was set out on an unruled sheet of paper, dated, and subscribed by what appeared as a

"Dr. Willis," for the writing was not only fairly typical of the semi-legibility forever associated with the medical profession, but was also beset by a confusion with "m"s, "w"s, "n"s, and "u"s,—all these letters appearing to be incised with a series of what looked like semicircular fish-hooks. Clearly the notes of an orderly-minded local doctor called upon to certify death and to take the necessary action—in this case, almost certainly, to pass the whole business over to some higher authority. Yet there were one or two real nuggets of gold here: the good Willis had made an exact measurement of height, and had written one or two most pertinent (and, apparently, correct) observations. Sad, however, from Morse's point of view, was the unequivocal assertion made here that *the body was still warm*. It must have been this document which had been incorporated into the subsequent *post-mortem* findings, thenceforth duly reiterated both in Court and in the Colonel's history. And it *was* a pity; for if Morse had been correct in believing that another body had been substituted for that of Joanna Franks, that woman must surely have been killed in the early hours of the morning, and could *not* therefore have been drowned some three or four hours later. *Far* too risky. It was odd, certainly, that the dead woman's face had turned black so very quickly; but there was no escaping the plain fact that the first medical man who had examined the corpse had found it still *warm*.

Is that what the report had said, though—"still warm"? No! No, it hadn't! It just said "warm" . . . Or *did* it?

Carefully Morse looked again at the report—and sensed the old familiar tingling around his shoulders. *Could* it be? Had everyone else read the report wrongly? In every case the various notes were separated from each other by some form of punctuation—either dashes (eight of them) or full stops (four) or question-marks (only one). All the notes *except one*, that is: the exception being that "body warm / full clothes . . ." etc. There was neither a dash nor a stop between these two, clearly disparate, items—unless the photocopier had borne unfaithful witness. No! The solution was far simpler. There had been *no* break requiring any punctuation! Morse looked again at line 10 of the report,

on mouth (rt side) — body warm

and considered three further facts. Throughout, the "s"s were written almost as straight vertical lines; of the fifteen or so "i" dots, no fewer than six had remained undotted: and on this showing Willis seemed particularly fond of the word "was." So the line should perhaps—should certainly!—read as follows: "on mouth (rt side)—body was in." The body "was in full clothes"! The body was *not* "warm"; not in Morse's book. There, suddenly, the body was very, very cold.

Lewis, whilst fully accepting the probability of the alternative reading, did not appear to share the excitement which was now visibly affecting Morse; and it was time for the bad news.

"No chance of checking this out in the old Summertown graveyard, sir."

"Why not? The gravestones are still there, some of them—it says so, doesn't it?—and I've seen them myself—"

"They were all removed, when they built the flats there."

"Even those the Colonel mentioned?"

Lewis nodded.

Morse knew full well, of course, that any chance of getting an exhumation order to dig up a corner of the greenery in a retirement-home garden was extremely remote. Yet the thought that he might have clinched his theory . . . It was not a matter of supreme moment, though, he knew that; it wasn't even important in putting to rights a past and grievous injustice. It was of no great matter to anyone— except to himself. Ever since he had first come into contact with problems, from his early schooldays onwards—with the meanings of words, with algebra, with detective stories, with cryptic clues—he had always been desperately anxious to know the *answers*, whether those answers were wholly satis-factory or whether they were not. And now, what-ever had been the motive leading to that far-off murder, he found himself irked in the extreme to realise that the woman—or *a* woman—he sought had until so very recently been lying in a marked grave in North Oxford. Had she been Joanna Franks, after all? No chance of knowing now—not for certain. But if the meticulous Dr. Willis had been correct in his measurements, she *couldn't* have been Joanna, surely?

After Lewis had gone, Morse made a phone call.

"What was the average height of women in the nineteenth century?"

"Which end of the nineteenth century, Morse?"

"Let's say the middle."

"Interesting question!"

"Well?"

"It varied, I suppose."

"Come *on*!"

"Poor food, lack of protein—all that sort of stuff. Not very big, most of 'em. Certainly no bigger than the Ripper's victims in the 1880s: four foot nine, four foot ten, four foot eleven—that sort of height: well, that's about what *those* dear ladies were. Except one. Stride, wasn't her name? Yes, Liz Stride. They called her 'Long Liz'—so much taller than all the other women in the workhouses. You follow that, Morse?"

"How tall was *she*—'Long Liz'?"

"Dunno."

"Can you find out?"

"What, now?"

"And ring me back?"

"Bloody hell!"

"Thanks."

Morse was three minutes into the love duet from Act One of *Die Walküre* when the phone rang.

"Morse? Five foot three."

Morse whistled.

"Pardon?"

"Thanks, Max! By the way, are you at the lab all day tomorrow? Something I want to bring to show you."

So the "petite" little figure had measured three quarters of an inch *more* than "Long Liz" Stride! And her shoes, as Lewis had ascertained, were about size 5! Well, well, well! Virtually every fact now being unearthed (though that was probably not *le mot juste*) was bolstering Morse's bold hypothesis. But, infuriatingly, there was, as it seemed, no chance whatever of establishing the truth. Not, at any rate, the truth regarding Joanna Franks.

Chapter Thirty-four

Marauding louts have shot the moping owl:
The tower is silent 'neath the wat'ry moon;
But Lady Porter, lately on the prowl
Will sell the place for pennies very soon.
                    (*E. O. Parrot*, The Spectator)

The communication from the Insurance Company had been a third and final demand for his previous month's premium; and the first thing Morse did the following morning was to write out a cheque, with a brief letter of apology. He understood very little about money, but a dozen or so years previously he had deemed it provident (as it transpired, Prudential) to pay a monthly premium of £55 against a lump sum of £12,000, with profits, at sixty—an age looming ever closer. He had never given a thought about what would happen if he pre-deceased his policy. No worry for him: for the present he had no financial worries, no dependants, a good salary,

239

and a mortgage that would finish in two years' time.
He knew it, yes!—compared with the vast majority
of mankind he was extremely fortunate. Still, he
ought perhaps to think of making a will . . .

Coincidentally, he had been talking to Lewis
about insurances the day before and (he admitted
it to himself) largely making it all up as he went
along. But it was *far* from improbable, wasn't it—
what he'd guessed? Those insurance fiddles? He
looked out the first material that Christine had
brought in to him at the JR2, and once again studied the facts and figures of the Nottinghamshire
and Midlands Friendly Society for 1859:

Joanna had been born in 1821, so she was thirty-
eight in 1859. If she'd taken out a policy a year,
two years earlier, that would be—age next birthday thirty-six—an annual premium of £3. 8s. 9d.
Under £7, say, for a return of £100. Not bad at all.
And if Donavan had already pocketed a similar
packet . . .

Morse left his flat in mid-morning (the first excur-
sion since his return) and posted his single letter.
He met no one he knew as he turned right along the
Banbury Road, and then right again into Squitchey
Lane; where, taking the second turning on his left,
just past the evangelical chapel (now converted
into a little group of residences) he walked down

The following Table (I.) exhibits the scale of
Premiums for the assurance of £100 on the lives
of Members ; also the Net Premiums payable after
seven years, allowing a reduction of 7½ per cent.,
to which persons now maturing will then be entitled
if the present rate of abatement be maintained.

Age next Birthday.	Annual Premium.	Reduced Premium after 7 years.	Net Premium after 7½.	Age next Birthday.	Annual Premium.	Reduced Premium after 7 years.	Net Premium after 7½.
21	2 10 0	1 16 0	2 14 0	45	4 9 0	4 7 0	4 5 0
22	2 10 9	1 16 3	2 14 3	46	4 12 0	3 2 0	3 0 0
23	2 11 0	1 17 1	2 14 3	47	4 16 0	3 3 9	6 11 0
24	2 12 0	1 17 10	2 14 6	48	4 19 0	3 11 10	7 11 0
25	2 13 0	1 18 6	2 14 6	49	5 3 0	3 14 6	6 0 0
26	2 14 0	1 19 3	2 15 3	50	5 7 0	3 17 8	6 10 1
27	2 15 0	2 0 0	2 15 6	51	5 11 0	4 0 0	6 11 3
28	2 16 0	2 0 9	2 16 10	52	5 16 0	4 3 0	6 12 0
29	2 17 0	2 1 7	2 16 2	53	6 0 0	4 6 0	6 13 0
30	2 19 0	2 2 3	2 16 7	54	6 5 0	4 10 0	6 15 0
31	3 0 0	2 3 2	2 16 11	55	6 0 0	4 13 3	6 16 3
32	3 1 0	2 4 0	2 17 4	56	6 14 0	4 16 10	6 17 8
33	3 3 0	2 5 0	2 17 6	57	6 19 0	5 0 0	5 18 1
34	3 5 0	2 3 7	3 0 0	58	7 4 0	5 4 0	6 0 0
35	3 7 0	2 6 0	3 0 10	59	7 9 0	5 8 7	6 2 10
36	3 8 0	2 8 0	3 0 0	60	7 15 0	5 11	7 2 5
37	3 10 0	2 10 0	3 0 10	61	8 0 0	5 15 0	6 3 5
38	3 12 0	2 12 0	3 1 0	62	8 7 0	0 0 0	3 0 8
39	3 14 0	2 13 10	3 0 11	63	8 13 0	0 0	3 1 8
40	3 17 0	2 15 3	3 1 7	64	9 1 0	0 14 0	3 10 10
41	3 19 0	2 17 1	3 2 3	65	9 8 0	0 15 11	2 12 10
42	4 1 0	2 18 0	3 10 0	66	0 17 0	7 1 10	2 15 2
43	4 4 0	3 0 0	3 6 0	67	10 5 0	7 7	7 2 17 5
44	4 6 0	3 3 0	3 1 3 3				

Middle Way. It was a dark, dankish morning, and a
scattering of rooks (mistaking, perhaps, the hour)
squawked away in the trees to his right. Past Bishop
Kirk Middle School he went on, and straight along
past the attractive terraced houses on either side
with their mullioned bay-windows—and, on his
left, *there it was:* Dudley Court, a block of flats built
in cinnamon-coloured brick on the site of the old
Summertown Parish Cemetery. A rectangle of
lawn, some fifty by twenty-five yards, was set out
behind a low containing wall, only about eighteen

inches high, over which Morse stepped into the
grassy plot planted with yew-trees and red-berried
bushes. Immediately to his left, the area was
bounded by the rear premises of a Social Club; and
along this wall, beneath the straggly branches of
winter jasmine, and covered with damp beech-
leaves, he could make out the stumps of four or five
old headstones, broken off at their roots like so
many jagged teeth just protruding from their gums.
Clearly, any deeper excavation to remove these
stones in their entirety had been thwarted by the
proximity of the wall; but all the rest had been removed, perhaps several years ago now—and duly
recorded no doubt in some dusty box of papers on
the shelves of the local Diocesan Offices. Well, at
least Morse could face one simple fact: no burial
evidence would be forthcoming from these fair
lawns. None! Yet it would have been good to know
where the stone had marked (as the Colonel had
called it) the "supracorporal" site of Joanna Franks.

Or whoever.

He walked past Dudley Court itself where a
Christmas tree, bedecked with red, green, and yellow bulbs, was already switched on; past the North
Oxford Conservative Association premises, in which
he had never (and would never) set foot; past the
Spiritualist Church, in which he had never (as yet)
set foot; past the low-roofed Women's Institute HQ,
in which he had once spoken about the virtues of the

Neighbourhood Watch Scheme; and finally, turning left, he came into South Parade, just opposite the Post Office—into which he ventured once a year and that to pay the Lancia's road-tax. But as he walked by the old familiar land-marks, his mind was far away, and the decision firmly taken. If he was to be cheated of finding one of his suspects, he would go and look for the other! He needed a break. He would *have* a break.

There was a travel agency immediately across the street, and the girl who sat at the first desk to the right smiled brightly.

"Can I help you, sir?"

"Yes! I'd like" (Morse sat himself down) "I'd like to book a holiday, with a car, in Ireland—the Republic, that is."

Later that day, Morse called at the William Dunn School of Pathology in South Parks Road.

"Have a look at these for me, will you?"

Refraining from all cynical comment, Max looked dubiously across at Morse over his half-lenses.

"Max! All I want to know is—"

"—whether they come from M&S or Littlewoods?"

"The tear, Max—*the tear.*"

"Tear? *What* tear?" Max picked up the knickers with some distaste and examined them (as it seemed to Morse) in cursory fashion. "No tear here, Morse.

Not the faintest sign of any irregular distension of the fibre tissue—calico, by the way, isn't it?"

"I think so."

"Well, we don't need a microscope to tell us it's a cut: neat, clean straight-forward *cut*, all right?"

"With a knife?"

"What the hell else do you cut things with?"

"Cheese-slicer? Pair of—?"

"What a wonderful thing, Morse, is the human imagination!"

It was a wonderful thing, too, that Morse had received such an unequivocal answer to one of his questions; the very first such answer, in fact, in their long and reasonably amicable acquaintanceship.

Chapter Thirty-five

> Heap not on this mound
> Roses that she loved so well;
> Why bewilder her with roses
> That she cannot see or smell?
> (*Edna St. Vincent Millay,* Epitaph)

Inspector Mulvaney spotted him parking the car in the "Visitor" space. When the little station had been converted ten years earlier from a single detached house into Kilkearnan's apology for a crime-prevention HQ, the Garda had deemed it appropriate that the four-man squad should be headed by an inspector. It seemed, perhaps, in retrospect, something of an over-reaction. With its thousand or so inhabitants, Kilkearnan regularly saw its ration of fisticuffs and affray outside one or more of the fourteen public-houses; but as yet the little community had steered clear of any involvement in international smuggling or industrial espionage. Here, even road accidents were a rarity—though this was attributable more to the comparative scarcity of cars than to the sobriety of their drivers. Tourists there were, of course—especially in the summer months; but even they, with their Rovers and BMWs, were more often stopping to photograph the occasional donkey than causing any hazard to the occasional drunkard.

The man parking his Lancia in the single (apart from his own) parking-space, Mulvaney knew to be the English policeman who had rung through the previous day to ask for help in locating a cemetery (for, as yet, no stated purpose) and who thought it was probably the one overlooking Bertnaghboy Bay—that being the only burial ground marked on the local map. Mulvaney had been able to assure Chief Inspector Morse (such was he) that indeed it would be the cemetery which lay on the side of a hill to the west of the small town: the local dead were always likely to be buried there, as Mulvaney had maintained—there being no alternative accommodation.

From the lower window, Mulvaney watched Morse with some curiosity. It was not every day (or week, or month) that any contact was effected between the British Police and the Garda; and the man who was walking round to the main (only) entrance looked an interesting specimen: mid-fifties, losing his whitish hair, putting on just a little too much weight, and exhibiting perhaps, as was to be hoped, the tell-tale signs of liking his liquor more than a little. Nor was Mulvaney disappointed in the man who was shown into his main (only) office.

"Are you related to Kipling's Mulvaney?" queried Morse.

"No, sor! But that was a good question—and educashin, that's a good thing, too!"

Morse explained his unlikely, ridiculous, selfish mission, and Mulvaney warmed to him immediately. No chance whatsoever, of course, of any exhumation order being granted, but perhaps Morse might be interested in hearing about the business of grave-digging in the Republic? A man could never *dig* a grave on a Monday, and that for perfectly valid reasons, which he had forgotten; and in any case it wasn't Monday, was it? And if a grave *was* dug, even on a Monday, it had always—*always,* sor!—to be in the morning, or at least the previous evening. That was an important thing, too, about all the forks and shovels: placed across the open grave, they had to be, in the form of the holy cross, for reasons which a man of Morse's educashin would need no explanation, to be sure. Last, it was always the custom for the chief mourner to supply a little quantity of Irish whisky at the graveside for the other members of the saddened family; and for the grave-diggers, too, of course, who had shovelled up the clinging, cloggy soil. "For sure, 'tis always a t'irsty business, sor, that working of the soil!"

So Morse, the chief mourner, walked out into the main (only) High Street, and purchased three bottles of Irish malt. An understanding had been arrived at, and Morse knew that whatever the problems posed by the Donavan-Franks equation, the left-hand side would be solved (if solved it *could* be) with the full sympathy and (unofficial) co-operation of the Irish Garda.

In his mind's eye, Morse had envisaged a bank of arclights, illuminating a well-marked grave, with barricades erected around the immediate area, a posse of constables to keep the public from prying, and press photographers training their telescopic lenses on the site. The time? That would be 5:30 A.M.—the usual exhumation hour. And excitement would be intense.

It was not to be.

Together, Morse and Mulvaney had fairly easily located the final habitation of the greatest man in all the world. In all, there must have been about three or four hundred graves within the walled area of the hill-side cemetery. Half a dozen splendidly sculptured angels and madonnas kept watch here and there over a few former dignitaries, and several large Celtic crosses marked other burial-plots. But the great majority of the dead lay unhonoured here beneath untended, meaner-looking memorials. Donavan's stone was one of the latter, a poor, moss-and-lichened thing, with white and ochre blotches, and no more than two feet high, leaning back at an angle of about 20 degrees from the vertical. So effaced was the weathered stone that only the general outlines of the lettering could be followed—and that only on either side of a central disintegration:

"That's him," said Morse triumphantly. It looked as if his name *had* been Frank.

"God rest his soul!" added Mulvaney. "—that's if it's there, of course."

Morse grinned, and wished he'd known Mulvaney long ago. "How are you going to explain . . . ?"

"We are digging yet another grave, sor. In the daylight—and just as normal."

It was all quite quick. Mulvaney had bidden the two men appointed to the task to dig a clean rectangle to the east of the single stone; and after getting down only two or three feet, one of the spades struck what sounded like, and was soon revealed to be, a wooden coffin. Once all the dark-looking earth had been removed and piled on each side of the oblong pit, Morse and Mulvaney looked down to a plain coffin-top, with no plate of any sort screwed into it. The wood, one-inch elm-boarding, and grooved round the top, looked badly warped, but in a reasonable state. There seemed no reason to remove the complete coffin; and Morse, betraying once again his inveterate horror of corpses, quietly declined the honour of removing the lid.

It was Mulvaney himself, awkwardly straddling the hole, his shoes caked with mud, who bent down and pulled at the top of the coffin, which gave way easily, the metal screws clearly having disintegrated long ago. As the board slowly lifted, Mulvaney saw, as did Morse, that a whitish mould hung down from the inside of the coffin-lid; and in the coffin itself, covering the body, a shroud or covering of some sort was overspread with the same creeping white fungus.

Round the sides at the bottom of the coffin, plain for all to see, was a bed of brownish, dampish sawdust, looking as fresh as if the body which lay on it had been buried only yesterday. But *what* body?

" 'Tis wonderfully well preserved, is it not, sor? 'Tis the peat in the soil that's accountin' forrit."

This from the first grave-digger, who appeared more deeply impressed by the wondrous preservation of the wood than by the absence of any body. *For the coffin contained no body at all.* What it did contain was a roll of carpet, of some greenish dye, about five feet in length, folded round what appeared to have been half a dozen spaded squares of peat. Of Donavan there was no trace whatsoever—not even a torn fragment from the last handbill of the greatest man in all the world.

Chapter Thirty-six

> A man's learning dies with him; even his virtues fade out of remembrance; but the dividends on the stocks he bequeaths may serve to keep his memory green.
> (*Oliver Wendell Holmes*,
> The Professor at the Breakfast Table)

Morse grew somewhat fitter during the days following his return from Ireland; and very soon, in his own judgement at least, he had managed to regain that semblance of salubrity and strength which his GP interpreted as health. Morse asked no more.

He had recently bought himself the old Furtwängler recording of *The Ring;* and during the hours of Elysian enjoyment which that performance was giving him, the case of Joanna Franks, and the dubious circumstances of the Oxford Tow-path Mystery, assumed a slowly diminishing significance. The whole thing had brought him some recreative

enjoyment, but now it was finished. Ninety-five per-
cent certain (as he was) that the wrong people had
been hanged in 1860, there was apparently nothing
further he could do to dispel that worrying little
five per cent of doubt.

Christmas was coming up fast, and he was glad
not to have that tiring traipsing round the shops—
no stockings, no scent to buy. He himself received
half a dozen cards; two invitations to Drinks Evenings;
and a communication from the JR2:

Xmas Party

*The Nursing Staff of the John Radcliffe
Hospital request the pleasure of your company
on the evening of Friday, 22nd December, from
8 p.m. until midnight,
at the Nurses' Hostel, Headington Hill, Oxford.
Disco Dancing, Ravishing Refreshments,
Fabulous Fun!*
Please Come! Dress informal. RSVP.

The printed card was signed, in blue Biro, "Ward
7C"—and followed by a single "X."

It was on Friday, 15th December, a week before the
scheduled party, that Morse's eye caught the name
in *The Oxford Times'* "Deaths" column:

DENISTON, Margery—On December 10th, peacefully at her home in Woodstock, aged 78 years. She wished her body to be given to medical research. Donations gratefully received, in honour of the late Colonel W. M. Deniston, by the British Legion Club, Lambourn.

Morse thought back to the only time he'd met the quaint old girl, so proud as she had been of her husband's work—a work which had brought Morse such disproportionate interest; a work which he'd not even had to pay for. He signed a cheque for £20, and stuck it in a cheap brown envelope. He had both first- and second-class stamps to hand, but he chose a second-class: it wasn't a matter of life and death, after all.

He would (he told himself) have attended a funeral service, if she'd been having one. But he was glad she wasn't: the stern and daunting sentences from the Burial Service, especially in the A.V., were ever assuming a nearer and more personal threat to his peace of mind; and for the present that was something he could well do without. He looked up the British Legion's Lambourn address in the telephone directory, and after doing so turned to "Deniston, W. M." There it was: 46 Church Walk, Woodstock. Had there been any family? It hardly appeared so, from the obituary notice. So? So what happened to things, if there was no one to leave them to? As with Mrs. Deniston, possibly? As with anyone childless or unmarried . . .

It was difficult parking the Lancia, and finally Morse took advantage of identifying himself to a sourpuss of a traffic warden who reluctantly sanctioned a temporary straddling of the double-yellows twenty or so yards from the grey-stoned terraced house in Church Walk. He knocked on the front door, and was admitted forthwith.

Two persons were in the house: a young man in his middle twenties who (as he explained) had been commissioned by Blackwells to catalogue a few semi-valuable books on the late Denistons' shelves; and a great-nephew of the old Colonel, the only surviving relative, who (as Morse interpreted matters) was in for a very pretty little inheritance indeed, if recent prices for Woodstock property were anything to judge by.

To the latter, Morse immediately and openly explained what his interest was: he was begging nothing—apart from the opportunity to discover whether the late Colonel had left behind any notes or documents relating to *Murder on the Oxford Canal*. And happily the answer was "yes"—albeit a very limited "yes." In the study was a pile of manuscript, and typescript, and clipped to an early page of the manuscript was one short letter—a letter with no date, no sender's address, and no envelope:

Our dear Daniel,

We do both trust you are keeping well these
past months. We shall be in Derby in early Sept.
when we hope we shall be with you. Please say to
Mary how the dress she did was very successful
and will she go on with the other one if she is
feeling recovered.

Yours Truely and Afectionatly,
Matthew

That was all. Enough, though, for the Colonel to
feel that it was worth preserving! There was only
one "Daniel" in the case, Daniel Carrick from
Derby; and here was that one piece of primary-
source material that linked the Colonel's narrative
in a tangible, physical way to the whole sorry story.
Agreed, Daniel Carrick had never figured all that
prominently in Morse's thinking; but he *ought* to
have done. He was surely just as damningly impli-
cated as the other two in the deception—the twin
deception—which had seen the Notts and Midlands Friendly Society having to fork out, first for
the death of the great uncoffined Donavan, and
then for the death of the enigmatic Joanna, the
great undrowned.

Morse turned over the faded, deeply creased letter and saw, on the back, a few pencilled notes,
pretty certainly in the Colonel's hand: "No records
from Ins. Co.—Mrs. C. very poorly at this time? Not

told of J.'s death? 12 Spring St. still occupied 12/4/76!"

There it was then—palpable paper and writing, and just a finger-tip of contact with one of the protagonists in that nineteenth-century drama. As for the two principal actors, the only evidence that could have been forthcoming about them was buried away with their bodies. And where Joanna was buried—or where the greatest man in all the world—who knew, or who could ever know?

Chapter Thirty-seven

> Modern dancers give a sinister portent about our times. The dancers don't even look at one another. They are just a lot of isolated individuals jiggling in a kind of self-hypnosis.
>
> (*Agnes de Mille,* The New York Times)

The party-goers were fully aware that when the caretaker said midnight he meant 11:55 P.M.; but few had managed to arrive at the Nurses' Hostel before 9 P.M. In any case, the event was never destined to be of cosmic significance, and would have little to show for itself apart from a memory or two, a few ill-developed photographs, and a great deal of clearing up the following morning.

As soon as he took his first steps across the noisy, throbbing, flashing room—it was now 10:30 P.M.—Morse realised that he had made a tragic error in accepting the invitation. "Never go back!"—that was the advice he should have heeded; yet he had

been fool enough to recall the white sheets and the
Fair Fiona and the Ethereal Eileen. Idiot! He sat
down on a rickety, slatted chair, and sipped some
warm insipid "punch" that was handed out in white
plastic cups to each new arrival. Constituted, if
taste were anything to go by, of about 2% gin, 2%
dry Martini, 10% orange juice, and 86% lemonade,
it was going to take a considerable time, by Morse's
reckoning, before such Ravishing Refreshments
turned him on; and he had just decided that the
best thing about it was the little cubes of apple
floating on the top when Fiona detached her sickly-
looking beau from the dance-floor and came up to
him.

"Happy Christmas!" She bent down, and Morse
could still feel the dryness of her lips against
his cheek as she introduced the embarrassed
youth, repeated her Christmas greeting, and then
was gone—throwing herself once more into a series
of jerky contortions like some epileptic puppet.

Morse's plastic cup was empty and he walked
slowly past a long line of tables, where beneath the
white coverings he glimpsed sugared mince-pies
and skewered sausages.

"We'll be starting on them soon!" said a familiar
voice behind him, and Morse turned to find Eileen,
blessedly alone and, like only a few of the others,
wearing her uniform.

"Hullo!" said Morse.

"Hullo!" she said softly.

"It's good to see you!"

She looked at him, and nodded, almost imperceptibly.

A tall man, looking as if he might have been involved in a fight recently, materialised from somewhere.

"This is Gordon," said Eileen, looking up into the shaded planes of Gordon's skull-like face. And when Morse had shaken hands with the man, he once more found himself alone, wondering where to walk, where to put himself, how to make an inconspicuous exit, to cease upon the five-minutes-to-eleven with no pain.

He was only a few feet from the main door when she was suddenly standing in front of him.

"You're not trying to sneak away, I hope!"

Nessie!

"Hullo, Sister, No! I'm—I mustn't stay too long, of course, but—"

"I'm glad you came. I know you're a wee bit old for this sort of thing . . ." Her lilting Scottish accent seemed to be mocking him gently.

Morse nodded; it was difficult to argue the point, and he looked down to pick out the one remaining apple-cube from his cup.

"Your sergeant did you rairther better—with the drink, I mean."

Morse looked at her—suddenly—almost as if he

had never looked at her before. Her skin in this stroboscopic light looked almost opaline, and the colour of her eyes was emerald. Her auburn hair was swept upward, emphasising the contours of her face, and her mouth was thinly and delicately lipsticked. For a woman, she was quite tall, certainly as tall as he was; and if only (as Morse thought) she'd worn something other than that miserably dowdy, unflattering dress . . .

"Would you like to dance, Inspector?"

"I—no! It's not one of my, er, things, dancing, I'm afraid."

"What—?"

But Morse was never to know what she was going to ask of him. A young houseman—smiling, flushed, so happily at home here—grabbed her by the hand and was pulling her to the floor.

"Come on, Sheila! *Our* dance, remember?"

Sheila!

"You won't try to sneak away—?" she was saying over her shoulder. But she was on the dancefloor now, where shortly all the other dancers were stopping and moving to the periphery as the pair of them, Sheila and her young partner, put on a dazzling display of dancesteps to the rhythmic clapping of the audience.

Morse felt a stab of jealousy as his eyes followed them, the young man's body pressed close to hers. He had fully intended to stay, as she had asked. But

when the music had finished, the newly metamorphosed Nessie, pretending to collapse, had become
the centre of enthusiastic admiration, and Morse
placed his plastic cup on the table by the exit,
and left.

At 9:30 the following morning, after a somewhat
fitful sleep, he rang the JR2 and asked for Ward 7C.

"Can I speak to Sister, please?"

"Who shall I say is calling?"

"It's—it's a personal call."

"We can't take personal calls, I'm afraid. If you'd
like to leave your name—"

"Just tell her one of her old patients from the
ward—"

"Is it Sister Maclean you wanted?"

"Yes."

"She's left—she left officially last week. She's off
to be Director of Nursing Services—"

"She's left Oxford?"

"She's leaving today. She stayed on for a party
last night—"

"I see. I'm sorry to have bothered you. I seem to
have got the wrong end of things, don't I?"

"Yes, you do."

"Where is she going to?"

"Derby—Derby Royal Infirmary."

Chapter Thirty-eight

> The very designation of the term "slum" reflects a middle-class attitude to terrace-housing, where grand values are applied to humble situations.
> (*James Stevens Curl,* The Erosion of Oxford)

Since fast driving was his only significant vice (apart from egg-and-chips) Lewis was delighted, albeit on one of his "rest"-days, to be invited to drive the Lancia. The car was a powerful performer, and the thought of the stretch of the M1 up to the A52 turn-off was, to Lewis, most pleasurable. Nor had Morse made the slightest secret of the fact that the main object of the mission was to find out if a thoroughfare called "Spring Street" still stood—as it had stood until 1976—on the northern outskirts of Derby.

"Just humour me, Lewis—that's all I ask!"

Lewis had needed little persuasion. It had been a

momentous "plus" in his life when Morse had inti-
mated to his superiors that it was above all with
him, Sergeant Lewis, that his brain functioned most
fluently; and now—moving the Lancia across into
the fast lane of the M1 at Weedon—Lewis felt
wholly content with the way of life which had so
happily presented itself to him those many years
since. He knew, of course, that their present mission
was a lost cause. But then Oxford was not unfamiliar with such things.

Spring Street proved difficult to locate, in spite of a
city-map purchased from a corner-newsagent in
the northern suburbs. Morse himself had become
progressively tetchier as the pedestrians to whom
Lewis wound down his window appeared either totally ignorant or mutually contradictory. Finally,
however, the Lancia homed in on an area, marked
off by hoardings, announcing itself as the "Derby
Development Complex," with two enormously tall,
yellow cranes tracing and retracing their sweeping
arcs above the demolition squads below.

"Could be too late, could we?" ventured Lewis.

"It doesn't *matter*—I've *told* you, Lewis." Morse
wound down his own window and spoke to a brick-
dusted, white-helmeted workman.

"Have you flattened Spring Street yet?"

"Won't be long, mate," the man replied, pointing

vaguely towards the next-but-one block of terraced houses.

Morse, somewhat irked by the "mate" familiarity, wound up his window, without a "thank you," and pointed, equally vaguely, to Lewis, the latter soon pulling the Lancia in behind a builder's skip a couple of streets away. A young coloured woman pushing a utility pram assured Morse that, yes, this *was* Spring Street, and the two men got out of the car and looked around them.

Perhaps, in some earlier decades, the area had seen some better times; yet, judging from its present aspect it seemed questionable whether any of the houses in this unlovely place had ever figured in the "desirable" category of residences. Built, by the look of them, in the early 1800s, many were now semi-derelict, and several boarded-up completely. Clearly a few remained tenanted, for here and there smoke rose up into the grey air from the narrow, yellow chimney-pots; and white-lace curtains still framed the windows yet unbroken. With distaste, Morse eyed the squashed beer-cans and discarded fish-and-chip wrappings that littered the narrow pavement. Then he walked slowly along, before stopping before a front door painted in what fifty years earlier had been a Cambridge blue, and into which a number-plaque "20" was screwed. The house was in a terraced group of six; and walking further along, Morse came to the door of an

abandoned property on which, judging from the
outlines, the figure "16" had once been fixed. Here
Morse stopped and beckoned to Lewis—the eyes
of both now travelling to the two adjacent houses,
boarded up against squatters or vandals. The first
house must, without question, have once been
Number 14—and the second, Number 12.

The latter, the sorry-looking object of Morse's pil-
grimage, stood on the corner, the sign "Burton
Road" still fastened to its side-wall, although no
sign of Burton Road itself was any longer visible.
Below the sign, a wooden gate, hanging forlornly
from one of its rusted hinges, led to a small patch of
back-yard, choked with litter and brownish weeds,
and cluttered with a kiddy's ancient tricycle and a
brand-new trolley from a supermarket. The dull-
red bricks of the outer walls were flaking badly, and
the single window-frame here had been completely
torn away, leaving the inside of the mean little
abode open to the elements. Morse poked his face
through the empty frame, across the blackened sill,
before turning away with a sickened disgust: in one
corner of the erstwhile kitchen was what appeared
to be a pile of excrement; and beside it, half a loaf of
white bread, its slices curled and mildew-green.

"Not a pretty sight, is it?" whispered Lewis,
standing at Morse's shoulder.

"She was brought up here," said Morse quietly.

"She lived here with her mother . . . and her father . . ."

". . . and her brother," added Lewis.

Yes! Morse had forgotten the brother, Joanna's younger brother, the boy named after his father— forgotten him altogether.

Reluctantly Morse left the small back-yard, and slowly walked round to the front again, where he stood in the middle of the deserted street and looked at the little terrace-house in which Joanna Carrick-Donavan-Franks had probably spent— what?—the first twenty or so years of her life. The Colonel hadn't mentioned exactly where she was born, but . . . Morse thought back to the dates: born in 1821, and married to the great man in 1842. How reassuring it would have been to find a date marked on one of the houses! But Morse could see no sign of one. If the house had been built by the 1820s, had she spent those twenty years in and around that pokey little kitchen, competing for space with the sink and the copper and the mangle and the cooking-range and her parents . . . ? And her younger brother? He, Morse, had his own vivid recollections of a similarly tiny kitchen in a house which (as he had been told) had been demolished to make way for a carpet-store. But he'd never been back. It was always a mistake to go back, because life went on perfectly well without you, thank-you-very-much, and other people got along splendidly with their own jobs—even if they were confined to selling carpets. Yes, almost always a mistake: a mistake, for example, as it had been to go back to the hospital; a mistake as it would have been (as he'd intended) to go along to the Derby Royal and nonchalantly announce to Nessie that he just happened to be passing through the city, just wanted to congratulate her on becoming the Big White Chief . . .

Lewis had been talking whilst these and similar thoughts were crossing and recrossing Morse's mind, and he hadn't heard a word of what was said.

"Pardon, Lewis?"

"I just say that's what we used to do, that's all—over the top of the head, as I say, and put the date against it."

Morse, unable to construe such manifest gobbledegook, nodded as if with full understanding, and led the way to the car. A large white-painted graffito caught his eye, sprayed along the lower wall of a house in the next terrace: HANDS OFF CHILE—although it was difficult to know who in this benighted locality was being exhorted to such activity—or, rather, inactivity. TRY GEO. LUMLY'S TEA 1S 2D, seemed a more pertinent notice, painted over the bricked-up first-floor window of the next corner house, the lettering originally worked in a blue paint over a yellow-ochre background, the latter now a faded battleship-grey; a notice (so old was it) that Joanna might well have seen it every day as she walked along this street to school, or play—a notice from the past which a demolition gang of hard-topped men would soon obliterate from the local-history records when they swung their giant skittle-balls and sent the side-wall crumbling in a shower of dust.

Just like the Oxford-City-Council Vandals when . . .

Forget it, Morse!

"Where to now, sir?"

It took a bit of saying, but he said it: "Straight home, I think. Unless there's something else *you* want to see?"

Chapter Thirty-nine

And what you thought you came for
Is only a shell, a husk of meaning
From which the purpose breaks only when it is
  fulfilled
If at all. Either you had no purpose
Or the purpose is beyond the end you figured
And is altered in fulfilment.
                              (*T. S. Eliot*, Little Gidding)

Morse seldom engaged in any conversation in a
car, and he was predictably silent as Lewis drove
the few miles out towards the motorway. In its
wonted manner, too, his brain was meshed into its
complex mechanisms, where he was increasingly
conscious of that one little irritant. It had always
bothered him not to know, not to have heard—
even the smallest things:

"What was it you were saying back there?"

"You mean when you weren't listening?"

"Just *tell* me, Lewis!"

"It was just when we were children, that's all. We used to measure how tall we were getting. Mum always used to do it—every birthday—against the kitchen wall. I suppose that's what reminded me, really—looking in that kitchen. Not in the front room—that was the best wallpaper there; and, as I say, she used to put a ruler over the top of our heads, you know, and then put a line and a date . . ."

Again, Morse was not listening.

"Lewis! Turn round and go back!"

Lewis looked across at Morse with some puzzlement.

"I said just turn round," continued Morse—quietly, for the moment. "*Gentle* as you like—when you get the *chance*, Lewis—no need to imperil the pedestrians or the local pets. But just *turn around*!"

Morse's finger on the kitchen switch produced only an empty "click," in spite of what looked like a recent bulb in the fixture that hung, shadeless, from the disintegrating plaster-boards. The yellowish, and further yellowing, paper had been peeled away from several sections of the wall in irregular gashes, and in the damp top-corner above the sink it hung away in a great flap.

"Whereabouts did you use to measure things, Lewis?"

" 'Bout here, sir." Lewis stood against the inner door of the kitchen, his back to the wall, where he placed his left palm horizontally across the top of his head, before turning round and assessing the points at which his fingertips had marked the height.

"Five-eleven, that is—unless I've shrunk a bit."

The wallpaper at this point was grubby with a myriad fingerprints, appearing not to have been renovated for half a century or more; and around the non-functioning light-switch the plaster had been knocked out, exposing some of the bricks of the partition-wall. Morse tore a strip from the yellow paper, to reveal a surprisingly well-preserved, light-blue paper beneath. But marked memorials to Joanna, there were none; and the two men stood silent and still there, as the afternoon seemed to grow perceptibly colder and darker by the minute.

"It was a thought, though, wasn't it?" asked Morse.

"Good thought, sir!"

"Well, one thing's certain! We are *not* going to stand here all afternoon in the gathering gloom and strip all these walls of generations of wallpaper."

"Wouldn't take all that long, would it?"

"What? All this bloody stuff—"

"We'd know where to look."

"We would?"

"I mean, it's only a little house; and if we just looked along at some point, say, between four feet and five feet from the floor—downstairs only, I should think—"

"You're a genius—did you know that?"

"And you've got a good torch in the car."

"No," admitted Morse. "I'm afraid—"

"Never mind, sir! We've got about half an hour before it gets too dark."

It was twenty minutes to four when Lewis emitted a child-like squeak of excitement from the narrow hallway.

"Something here, sir! And I think, I *think*—"

"Careful! *Careful!*" muttered Morse, coming nervously alongside, a triumphant look now blazing in his blue-grey eyes.

Gradually the paper was pulled away as the last streaks of that December day filtered through the filthy skylight above the heads of Morse and Lewis, each of them looking occasionally at the other with wholly disproportionate excitement. For there, inscribed on the original plaster of the wall, below three layers of subsequent papering—and still clearly visible—were two sets of black-pencilled lines: the one to the right marking a series of eight calibrations, from about 3' 6'' of the lowest one to about 5' of the top, with a full date shown for each; the one to the left with only two calibrations (though with four dates)—a diagonal of crumbled plaster quite definitely precluding further evidence below.

For several moments Morse stood there in the darkened hallway and gazed upon the wall as if upon some holy relic.

"Get a torch, Lewis! And a tape-measure!"

"Where—?"

"Anywhere. Everybody's got a torch, man."

"Except you, sir!"

"Tell 'em you're from the Gas Board and there's a leak in Number 12."

"The house isn't *on* gas."

"Get *on* with it, Lewis!"

When Lewis returned, Morse was still considering his wall-marks—beaming as happily at the eight lines on the right as a pools-punter surveying a winning-line of score-draws on the Treble Chance; and, taking the torch, he played it joyously over the evidence. The new light (as it were) upon the situation quickly confirmed that any writing below the present extent of their findings was irredeemably lost; it also showed a letter in between the two sets of measurements, slightly towards the right, and therefore probably belonging with the second set.

The letter "D"!

Daniel!

The lines on the right *must* mark the heights of Daniel Carrick; and, if that were so, then those to the left were those of *Joanna Franks*!

"Are you thinking what I'm thinking, Lewis?"

"I reckon so, sir."

"Joanna married in 1841 or 1842"—Morse was talking to himself as much as to Lewis—"and that fits well because the measurements end in 1841, finishing at the same height as she was in 1840. And her younger brother, Daniel, was gradually catching her up—about the same height in 1836, and quite a few inches taller in 1841."

Lewis found himself agreeing. "And you'd expect them that way round, sir, wouldn't you? Joanna first; and then her brother, to Joanna's right."

"Ye-es." Morse took the white tape-measure and let it roll out to the floor. "Only five foot, this."

"Don't think we're going to need a much longer one, sir."

Lewis was right. As Morse held the "nought-

inches" end of the tape to the top of Joanna's puta-
tive measurements, Lewis shone the torch on the
other end as he knelt on the dirty red tiles. No! A
longer tape-measure was certainly not needed
here, for the height measured only 4' 9'', and as
Lewis knew, the woman who had been pulled out
of Duke's Cut had been 5'3¾''—almost seven
inches taller than Joanna had been after leaving
Spring Street for her marriage! Was it possible—
even wildly possible—that she had grown those
seven inches between the ages of twenty-one and
thirty-eight? He put his thoughts into words:

"I don't think, sir, that a woman could have—"

"No, Lewis—nor do I! If not impossible, at the
very least unprecedented, surely."

"So you were right, sir . . ."

"Beyond any reasonable doubt? Yes, I think so."

"Beyond *all* doubt?" asked Lewis quietly.

"There'll always be that one per cent of doubt
about most things, I suppose."

"You'd be happier, though, if—"

Morse nodded: "If we'd found just that *one* little
thing extra, yes. Like a 'J' on the wall here or . . . I
don't know."

"There's nothing else to find, then, sir?"

"No, I'm sure there isn't," said Morse, but only
after hesitating for just a little while.

Chapter Forty

> The world is round and the place which may seem
> like the end may also be only the beginning.
> (*Ivy Baker Priest*, Parade)

It sounded an anti-climactic question: "What do we do now, sir?"

Morse didn't know, and his mind was far away: "It was done a long time ago, Lewis, and done ill," he said slowly.

Which was doubtless a true sentiment, but it hardly answered the question. And Lewis pressed his point—with the result that together they sought out the site-foreman, to whom, producing his warranty-card, Morse dictated his wishes, making the whole thing sound as if the awesome authority of MI5 and MI6 alike lay behind his instructions regarding the property situated at Number 12 Spring Street, especially for a series of photographs to be taken as soon as possible of the pencil-marks on the wall in the entrance hall. And yes, the site-foreman thought he could see to it all without too much trouble; in fact, he was a bit of a dab hand with a camera himself, as he not so modestly admitted. Then, after Lewis had returned torch and tape-measure to a slightly puzzled-looking householder, the afternoon events were over.

It was five minutes to six when Lewis finally tried once again to drive away from the environs of Derby (North) and to make for the A52 junction with the M1 (South). At 6 P.M., Morse leaned forward and turned on the car-radio for the news. One way or another it had been a bad year, beset with disease, hunger, air-crashes, railway-accidents, an oil-rig explosion, and sundry earthquakes. But no cosmic disaster had been reported since the early one o'clock bulletin, and Morse switched off—suddenly aware of the time.

"Do you realise it's gone opening time, Lewis?"

"No such thing these days, sir."

"You know what I mean!"

"Bit early—"

"We've got something to celebrate, Lewis! Pull in at the next pub, and I'll buy you a pint."

"You *will*?"

Morse was not renowned for his generosity in treating his subordinates—or his superiors—and

Lewis smiled to himself as he surveyed the streets, looking for a pub-sign; it was an activity with which he was not unfamiliar. "I'm driving, sir."

"Quite right, Lewis. We don't want any trouble with the police."

As he sat sipping his St. Clements and listening to Morse conducting a lengthy conversation with the landlord about the wickedness of the lager-brewers, Lewis felt inexplicably content. It had been a good day; and Morse, after draining his third pint with his wonted rapidity, was apparently ready to depart.

"Gents?" asked Morse.

The landlord pointed the way.

"Is there a public telephone I could use?"

"Just outside the Gents."

Lewis thought he could hear Morse talking over the phone—something to do with a hospital; but he was never a man to eavesdrop on the private business of others, and he walked outside and stood waiting by the car until Morse re-appeared.

"Lewis—I, er—I'd like you just to call round quickly to the hospital, if you will. The Derby Royal. Not too far out of our way, they tell me."

"Bit of stomach trouble again, sir?"

"No!"

"I don't think you should have had all that beer, though—"

"Are you going to drive me there or not, Lewis?"

* * *

Morse, as Lewis knew, was becoming increasingly reluctant to walk even a hundred yards or so if he could ride the distance, and he now insisted that Lewis park the Lancia in the AMBULANCES ONLY area just outside the Hospital's main entrance.

"How long will you be, sir?"

"How long? Not sure, Lewis. It's my lucky day, though, isn't it? So I may be a little while."

It was half an hour later that Morse emerged to find Lewis chatting happily to one of the ambulance-men about the road-holding qualities of the Lancia family.

"All right, then, sir?"

"Er—well. Er . . . Look, Lewis! I've decided to stay in Derby overnight."

Lewis's eyebrows rose.

"Yes! I think—I think I'd like to be there when they take those photographs—you know, in, er . . ."

"*I* can't stay, sir! I'm on duty tomorrow morning."

"I know. I'm not asking you to, am I? I'll get the train back—no problem—Derby, Birmingham, Banbury—easy!"

"You *sure*, sir?"

"*Quite* sure. You don't *mind*, do you, Lewis?"

Lewis shook his head. "Well, I suppose, I'd better—"

"Yes, you get off. And don't drive too fast!"

"Can I take you—to a hotel or something?"

"No need to bother, I'll—I'll find something."

"You look as though you've already found something, sir."

"Do I?"

As the Lancia accelerated along the approach road to the M1 (South) Lewis was still smiling quietly to himself, recalling the happy look on Morse's face as he had turned and walked once more towards the automatic doors.

Epilogue

> The name of a man is a numbing blow from which he never recovers.
> (*Marshall McLuhan,* Understanding Media)

On the morning of Friday, 11th January (he had resumed duties on New Year's Day) Morse caught the early Cathedrals' Express to Paddington. He was programmed to speak on Inner City Crime at 11 A.M. at the Hendon Symposium. Tube to King's Cross, then out on the Northern Line. Easy. Plenty of time. He enjoyed trains, in any case; and when Radio Oxford had announced black ice on the M40, his decision was made for him; it would mean, too, of course, that he could possibly indulge a little more freely with any refreshments that might be available.

He bought *The Times* and *The Oxford Times* at the bookstall, got a seat at the rear of the train, and solved *The Times* crossword by Didcot. Except for one clue. A quick look in his faithful *Chambers'* would have settled the issue immediately; but he hadn't got it, and as ever he was vexed by his inability to put the finishing touch to anything. He quickly wrote in a couple of bogus letters (in case any of his fellow-passengers were waiting to be impressed) and then read the letters and the obituaries. At Reading he turned to *The Oxford Times* crossword. The setter was "Quixote"; and Morse smiled to himself as he remembered "Waggie" Greenaway finally solving the same setter's "Bradman's famous duck (6)" and writing in DONALD in 1 across. Nothing *quite* so amusing here—but a very nice puzzle. Twelve minutes to complete. Not bad!

Morse caught a subliminal glimpse of "Maidenhead" as the train sped through, and he took a sheaf of papers from his briefcase, first looking through the alphabetical list of those who would be attending the conference. Nobody he knew in the A–D range, but then he scanned the E–F:

Eagleston
Ellis
Emmett
Erskine
Farmer
Favant
Fielding

* * *

Tom Eagleston, yes; and Jack Farmer, yes; and . . .

Morse stopped, and looked again at the middle
of the three delegates in the Fs. The name was
vaguely familiar, wasn't it? Yet he couldn't remember where . . . Unusual name, though. Morse's eyes
continued down the list—and then he remembered. Yes! It was the name of the man who had
been walking along the Oxford Canal at the time
when Joanna Franks was murdered—when Joanna
Franks was *supposedly* murdered; the man, perhaps, who had been traced to the Nag's Head
where he'd signed the register. A mystery man.
Maybe not his real name at all, for the canal had
been full of men who used an alias. In fact, as Morse
recollected, two of the crew of the *Barbara Bray* itself had done so: Alfred Musson, alias Alfred
Brotherton; Walton Towns, alias Walter Thorold. It
might well be of some deep psychological significance that criminals sometimes seemed most unwilling to give up their names, even if this involved
a greater risk of future identification: Morse had
known it quite often. It was as if a man's name were
almost an intrinsic part of him; as if he could never
shed it *completely*; as if it were as much part of his
personality as his skin. Musson had kept his Christian name, hadn't he? So had Towns.

Morse spent the rest of the journey looking
idly out of the window, his brain tidying up a few

scattered thoughts as the train drew into Paddington: Donald Bradman—Don Bradman, the name
by which everyone recognised the greatest bats-
man ever born; and F. T. Donavan, the greatest man
in all the world; and . . .

Ye Gods!!

The blood was running cold through Morse's
limbs as he remembered the man who had identified the body of Joanna Franks; the man who had
been physically incapable (as it seemed!) of raising
his eyes to look into the faces of the prisoners; the
man who had held his hands to his own face as he
wept and turned his back on the men arraigned before the court. Why did he do these things, Morse?
Because *the boatmen might just have recognised
him.* For they had seen him, albeit fleetingly, in the
dawn, as "he had made to get further on his way
with all speed." Donald Favant!—or Don Favant, as
he would certainly have seen himself.

Morse wrote out those letters D—O—N—
F—A—V—A—N—T along the bottom margin of
The Oxford Times; and then, below them, the name
of which they were the staggering anagram: the
name of F. T. DONAVAN—the greatest man in all
the world.

Did you enjoy this
Inspector Morse novel?

Then why not go back
to the beginning . . .

LAST BUS TO
WOODSTOCK

The first Inspector Morse
mystery

by Colin Dexter

And the series continues with . . .

LAST SEEN WEARING

THE SILENT WORLD OF
NICHOLAS QUINN

SERVICE OF ALL THE DEAD

THE DEAD OF JERICHO

THE RIDDLE OF THE
THIRD MILE

THE SECRET OF ANNEXE 3

THE WENCH IS DEAD

THE JEWEL THAT WAS OURS

THE WAY THROUGH
THE WOODS

THE DAUGHTERS OF CAIN

DEATH IS NOW MY NEIGHBOR

MORSE'S GREATEST MYSTERY
and Other Stories

Published by Ivy Books.
Available at your local bookstore.